All In

SUSAN HAYES

When love is the prize, the only way to win is to go all in.

The Resource Wars may have ended, but for the cyborgs created to fight in them, the battle for acceptance is far from over. Former soldiers Toro and Jaeger have been on the move since they left military service. They're looking for more than their next payday; they want to find a place to call home.

Cynder Armas co-owns the Nova Club with her two cyborg siblings. The club is more than her business; it's her home— filled with everyone she cares about. Life on The Drift isn't easy, but it is profitable, and it keeps her too busy to dwell on the losses in her past.

When these three battle-scarred warriors meet, there's no denying their attraction, but it takes more than a spark to keep a fire burning. To hold onto each other, they'll have to find a way to let go of their old lives and embrace the future, together.

COPYRIGHT

ALL IN
Author: Susan Hayes

ALL RIGHTS RESERVED: This literary work may not be reproduced or transmitted in any form or by any means, including electronic or photographic reproduction, in whole or in part, without express written permission.

All characters and events in this book are fictitious. Any resemblance to actual persons living or dead is strictly coincidental. It is fiction so facts and events may not be accurate except to the current world the book takes place in.

DEDICATION

For my parents, I wouldn't be here without your love and constant support as I chase after my dreams. For my best friend in the whole world, Karen, who lets me ramble on about the voices in my head and almost never laughs at me.

This book is also dedicated to Sadie Haller. Thank you for your advice, your friendship, and for making the best coffee on the planet.

Table of Contents

PROLOGUE

Out on the edge of civilized space lies a rag-tag collection of space stations and platforms known as the Drift. It's a haven for the hunted, the lost, and those seeking second chances. The ones who live there hail from every species, class, and corner of the galaxy, but they all have one thing in common: they don't belong anywhere else.

There's nothing beyond the Drift but wild space and an asteroid belt full of ore-rich rocks. Hundreds of mining vessels and their hard-working crews mine the asteroids. When the ships deliver their haul to be processed, those crews hit the infamous bars, casinos, and pleasure houses that are the Drift's primary source of income…and the only source of entertainment.

It's a world of its own. One where corporations rule, the laws are flexible, and everything is for sale, for the right price.

Welcome to the Drift.

CHAPTER ONE

Cynder paced back and forth in front of the door, listening to the crowd on the other side. It was another full house tonight in her bar, the Nova Club. A packed club meant profits were up, the liquor was flowing, and the betting would be fast and furious. Better yet, some of those bets would be on her performance in the ring tonight. Anyone who bet against her was going home poorer. There was no way in hell she was going to lose.

The door opened, and she was hit by a wall of noise. Her batch sibling, Kit, who was also one of the club's co-owners, stuck his head in and grinned at her. "You ready to kick ass?"

"You have no idea how much," she replied. She glanced past him, looking into the club. They had to be near their occupancy limit. Perfect. The energy of the crowd was a tangible thing: a heady blend of body heat, bloodlust, and booze-fueled enjoyment that hit her like a spike of adrenaline.

Kit cleared his throat, drawing her attention back to him. "Nothing like doing the month-end books to get you in the right frame of mind to go a few rounds, right? This time, can you please remember that your opponents aren't the enemy; they're contracted employees? Try not to break off anything vital."

She rolled her eyes at him, her thoughts already on the match to come. "I have never broken anything *off* of anyone, vital or otherwise. And before you even say it, a Jeskyran's body thorns grow back, so that one doesn't count."

Kit scoffed. "The way he was complaining and wailing? I'm betting he'd argue with your assessment. You stay sharp out there and good luck."

"I don't need luck tonight. Not unless Frey has suddenly stopped dropping his guard and Jester learned not to telegraph his moves."

"Don't get cocky. Cocky gets you dead," he said, using a line he had uttered a thousand times on the battlefield. They might have left that life behind, and Kit wasn't her commanding officer anymore, but some things were too ingrained to ever truly be forgotten.

She snapped off a salute in response and grinned at him. "Yessir, Major sir."

"Why do I put up with your sass again?" he asked.

"Because I'm your batch sister, your business partner, and the only person you know who can do the club's books. Also, I'm cute as hell and your wife thinks I'm awesome."

There was no mistaking the look of contentment that came over Kit's face the second she mentioned his wife, Zura. Kit and his brother had married the love of their lives three months ago, and the honeymoon phase was still going strong. The way the three of them looked at each other, Cyn suspected it would never end. Kit and his cloned twin, Luke, were deeply in love with Zura, and she felt the same about them. It was almost enough to make someone believe in true love and fairytales. *Almost.*

The noise of the crowd rose to a deafening roar, a sure sign that the fight before hers had come to an end.

"You're on in two minutes. We're introducing your opponents first. Fight smart, Cyn. I'll see you ringside." Kit tapped his fist to hers before leaving.

Once the door closed, the noise faded. Like all cyborgs, she had excellent hearing, vision, and other senses. They had been gifts without price when she was a soldier, but now that life was over, there were times she wished her enhancements had an off-switch, or at the very least, volume control.

She bounced on her toes and rolled her shoulders, loosening up in anticipation of stepping into the ring. The fight wouldn't be easy, but she knew it was winnable. It was part of the Nova Club's draw: each bout would be between well-matched opponents, and none of the fights were easy wins. It kept the betting hot and made sure everyone brought their A-game.

The habits of a lifetime kept her breathing slow and her heart rate steady even as she felt the familiar tingle of adrenaline. This was what she lived for now— these few, fleeting moments when she could focus on the present instead of the past. The brief stretches when she could exist one heartbeat at a time, reacting instead of remembering.

The door opened, and the maddening noise of the crowd rolled over her. Head up, hands high, she made her way to the ring, laughing every step of the way.

* * * *

Jaeger had only been in the Nova Club for an hour, but he could already see it was everything he had heard it was, and then some. The clientele was rough, the food was way above average for the Drift, and the drinks weren't watered down at all. The fights were fair, and the casino was well-run and above board. After spending two months working their way through half the bars, gambling dens, and fight clubs on the corporation-run platforms and stations that made up the Drift, the Nova was a welcome change of pace.

"Did you see the menu? They've got *fraxxing* grass-fed beef. Steak, Jaeg. When's the last time we had real, planet-raised meat, never mind a steak?"

Toro asked, tapping the menu with a thick finger for emphasis.

"Where the hell are they getting beef from out here? Check the fine print, there has to be a catch."

Toro scanned the menu again and then shook his head. "No catch. It says it's certified, colony-raised beef. I'm ordering it. I don't care if it wipes out my savings. It's *steak*!"

"And how many fights are you going to have to win before you can eat again? We're living lean these days." That was a slight exaggeration of their financial status, but not by much. If the Nova Club signed Toro on as a fighter, the signing bonus alone would ensure they could make ends meet until Toro won a fight or Jaeger hit a lucky streak at the gambling tables.

His best friend scowled at the reminder of their status. "We wouldn't be in the red if the last place we worked hadn't been run by a couple of thieving, conniving cowards. You won that money, and they had no right taking it back. Everyone knows starburst is an un-cheatable game, that's why it's so damned hard to win. We're cyborgs, not magicians with the ability to manipulate odds and gravity."

"That's why we're here. If there's any place on the Drift where no one is going to hassle us for being what we are, it's in a club run by other cyborgs. They know better than anyone in the galaxy what we're capable of," Jaeger said.

"I hope so. If this place pans out, I'd like to stick around for a while. I'm getting tired of sleeping in a new bed every few nights. It's starting to feel like we never left military service at all."

"At least the food's better," Jaeger commented as he finally read over the menu and winced at the prices. This far from civilization, everything was more expensive. It was another reminder that they needed to start making money soon. From what he had seen of the gaming tables, the Nova Club ran an honest game, which meant with a little luck, he should be able to turn their fortunes around in a week or less.

"Does this mean you're going to let loose and actually indulge in a steak with me? Come on, take a walk on the wild side." Toro was grinning as he waved over one of the serving staff.

"Like you said, it's *steak*. I'm in. Tomorrow, when we're both broke and hungry, remind me that giving in to temptation is never a good idea."

Toro shook his head. "Not a chance. You know those words will never pass my lips. Temptation is fun, and life is all about having fun and taking risks. You're a damned gambler; you know all about risk and reward."

"I know about carefully calculated risks and return on investment. That's not the same thing."

"Says the man about to order himself a big, juicy steak. Admit it, sometimes it feels good to give in to temptation." Toro turned to their server and flashed the young man a smile. "My buddy and I will both have the steak. Rare. Oh, and one of every side dish, and two more beers."

"You got it. You won't regret the steak; it's incredible. I got to try some the first time it came in, and it's worth the scrip."

"It better be," Jaeger muttered and pointed at Toro. "You need an impressive winning streak if you want to keep eating this way."

The server perked up at that. "You're a fighter? Have you signed on here? If you have, you get a discount on food and beverages."

"Not yet. Got a meeting with one of the owners a little later. We thought we'd come by and check the place out and watch the fights."

"You came on a good night. Cynder is on the roster. In fact, her fight is up next. I'm going to put in your order and go watch. I'll bring your steaks out as soon as they're ready."

"Cynder—hey, isn't that the name of the owner we're supposed to meet up with later?" Toro asked.

"Cynder Armas, yeah. If she's one of the owners, that's good news for us. It means they let cyborgs fight here. I know they agreed to talk to you, but that's never a sure sign."

"And there you go, being all practical again. I was hoping she was hot. I love a woman who knows how to fight dirty, if you know what I mean."

Jaeger rolled his eyes. "Keep thoughts like that to yourself, will you? You're not half as charming as you think you are, and we need her to sign you on as a fighter, not toss us out of here because you hit on her. She's going to be your boss, remember?"

He took a drink out of his mug before continuing. "Besides, one of has to be logical. Otherwise, we'd be broke and working a yearlong contract on some miserable mining ship somewhere out in that field of broken space rocks," he said, gesturing vaguely toward the windows and the asteroid field that filled much of the inner part of this solar system.

Toro frowned and dropped his gaze to his beer. "I know you're smarter than me. It's just...you can't be practical all the time. We survived the war, but sometimes I wonder if you're ever going to put that nightmare behind you and start really living."

"I'm trying. I ordered the damned steak, didn't I?" Jaeger pointed out. This was an old argument between the two of them. Jaeger played the part of the charming and laid-back gambler because it put people at ease, but most of it was an act. He had been that person once, but years of wartime service had darkened his soul. Toro kept hoping the old version of Jaeger would come back one day, but Jaeger didn't know if that man even existed anymore.

"Yeah, you did. I'm amazed a host of angels didn't break out in song the second it happened."

"Ass."

"Jerk."

The name-calling might have continued until their food arrived, but their insults were interrupted by a louder than average cheer from the crowd surrounding the fight ring. Toro winced as he took in the scene, and Jaeger twisted in his seat to check out what had his batch brother looking so pained. The match had ended, and from the looks of things, the loser's next stop would be the station's medical bay. His left arm hung at his side, and his shoulder was misshapen, both telltale signs of a dislocation.

"That's got to hurt," Toro muttered, rolling his own shoulders in sympathy.

"Thank you, corporate lab monkeys for giving us the ability to turn off pain receptors. On the plus side, I do believe an opening just appeared on the club's fight roster."

"It looks like it. A silver lining for us, not so much for that poor guy." Toro reached for his glass and then froze as the crowd started to cheer even louder.

The cheer turned into a chant. One word repeated over and over again. Sinner—no. It took Jaeger a few seconds to figure it out. Not sinner, Cynder. Curious, he settled back to watch the next fight. He hadn't seen a cyborg woman fight since the Resource Wars ended. In fact, he hadn't seen many of them, period. The corporations who had created and owned their cyborg soldiers had made most of their forces male. The exact ratio had varied from corporation to corporation, but as far as he had been able to determine, none of the groups had made more than thirty percent of their soldiers female. According to the official records, less than ten percent of all cyborgs had survived the wars and were eventually freed.

There weren't many of his kind left.

That was one of the reasons they'd made their way to the Drift. What few cyborgs remained seemed to be out here on the edge of civilized space. The Drift was unique in the galaxy. It existed on the edge of a massive asteroid field, beyond the territory of any race or government. The corporations who won the Resource Wars owned and ran the collection of stations and platforms that made up the Drift. They controlled everything from the contracts assigned to the deep space mining vessels, down to the air they all breathed. If the companies could find a way to profit from it, they did. It wasn't the easiest place to live, but it had its benefits, most notably the fact that acceptance came a little easier than anywhere else he and Toro had been. Maybe out here they would finally find a place where they belonged.

Toro watched the crowd around the ring with keen interest. An observant person could tell a lot about a venue by the kind of customers they attracted. The Nova Club was an interesting mix of hard cases and higher-class folks. There was a whole lot of money in play on the betting floor, but so far, everyone had been relatively well behaved. Their manners were, no doubt, due to the presence of several ever-vigilant security guards who moved through the crowd every few minutes. They kept the roughnecks from getting too rowdy, which meant the management types felt safe. It was a tricky balancing act, but done right, it made for bigger profits and a safer experience for everyone.

The chanting died down as the next two fighters were announced. Neither of them was named Cynder though. He started to wonder if their server had been mistaken about who would be fighting next. It wasn't until the two men entered the ring and went to the same corner that he caught on. They weren't fighting each other. They were both going to be fighting a third opponent.

The announcer started his introduction, but he had no chance of being heard over the excited cheers of the crowd that only got louder as *she* stepped into view.

Re'veth. She was breathtaking. Tall and lean, with long legs and the grace of a predator, the woman made her way to the ring. She laughed as she walked, though he couldn't hear her over the roar of the crowd as they welcomed their favorite fighter back. He couldn't take his eyes off of her.

"Now that's one hot woman," he murmured. Surprisingly, Jaeger agreed.

"Yes, she is."

For the second time tonight, Toro half expected angels to start singing. First, steak and now Yeager was actually noticing an attractive woman? Miracles abounded.

"Did you see the smile on her face? She loves this. The fighting, the rush, all of it."

Jaeger scoffed. "Which means she's as crazy as you are. Maybe crazier since she's an owner and is clearly making enough money she doesn't have to fight. She's in there because she wants to be. That's a special kind of lunatic."

"I know. I think I'm a little in love with her already, and we haven't even said hello yet," Toro said, still fixated on the beautiful warrior as she entered the ring.

"She's probably married to the other owners. They're supposed to be cloned twins, right? Get your mind out of the bedroom and back in the game. The match is about to start, and if we're lucky, you might be fighting one of these guys soon."

"I'm watching. I can multi-task, you know."

"Prove it, what color are her opponents wearing?" Jaeger asked.

"One's in green and white, the other's wearing red. She's in blue and silver, and judging by the décor in here, that's the club's official color scheme," Toro replied before flipping his middle finger up at his best friend. He might have been created to be cannon fodder, but even basic models like him were given enough brains to be able to track the smallest detail of their surroundings at all times. He wasn't the fastest or the smartest cyborg ever created, but he was a fighter, one who had survived almost a decade of battle.

"Hey, you know I was only giving you a hard time, right?" Jaeger asked.

Toro turned to face his friend. "Yeah, I know. It's just…" he shrugged. People had treated him like an idiot for the first ten years of his life. Everyone from the lab monkeys who'd help create him, to his commanding officers, to some of his fellow soldiers had assumed he was all brawn and no brain.

"I know. How about I make it up to you by letting you get in a few good hits the next time we spar?" Jaeger offered.

Toro laughed. "Like I need you to *let* me smack you. Over ten years since you came out of the maturation tank and you still can't dodge worth shit. It's a miracle you lived through the war, my friend."

"I wouldn't have if you hadn't saved my ass."

"Which time?" he raised his glass to his batch brother and best friend.

"All of 'em."

A bell sounded, and his attention swung back to the fight. Their seats were close enough he could see the action, but he wanted to get closer. He wanted to watch Cynder in action and see if she was as good as he suspected. Up against two men, she had to be.

"I'll be back after the fight. I want to see this," he said, rising from the table.

"If you're not back by the time your steak gets here, I'll assume you suddenly became a vegetarian and eat yours for you."

"Touch my dinner and I'll have to hurt you. I won't be gone long. If the food arrives before I do, send me a message." Toro tapped his temple. All cyborgs were created in batches and left their maturation tanks at the same time. Batch siblings trained and fought together. They all shared a certain amount of DNA, and they were linked together by internal communications. He and Jaeger still shared an internal comm-channel. At one time, all of their siblings had been part of the network, but now it was only the two of them.

He headed toward the ring, using his size to push through the crowd until he was right where he wanted to be. Close enough to see every move, but far enough back to still be able to watch the whole ring instead of only a piece of it. Hopefully, he would be facing off against these fighters someday soon, and he wanted to get a look at their tactics.

He didn't get much time to observe. The fight came to an abrupt end within a few minutes. The two matched up against Cynder weren't working together. Instead of keeping their opponent pressed and off-balance, they kept trying to take her on one-on-one, and it cost them the match.

Her speed was impressive, and she moved with such precision and grace it was obvious she had been created for something other than straight melee fighting. He couldn't be sure, but she was probably designed for stealth or infiltration of some kind. The gleam in her eyes as she fought told him that whatever her original purpose might have been, she was a kindred spirit when it came to fighting in the ring.

He had always hoped that one day he might find a woman who could accept his love of fighting. Never once had he considered he might actually meet a woman who felt the same thrill. Not until tonight.

Cynder finished off her last opponent with a roundhouse kick that sent him crashing to the mat. The crowd roared in approval while all around him scrip changed hands as bets were settled. The moment she was declared the winner, the fire faded from Cynder's eyes, and she went over to check on the man she had knocked out. Toro watched in surprise as she helped carry the injured man out of the cage. Despite her gift for violence, she still had her compassion.

Tonight was full of surprises.

He made it back to the table a few seconds before their meals arrived, complete with fresh mugs of beer.

"Good fight," Jaeger said.

"It could have been better if they'd worked together instead of letting their egos get in the way. They made it easy for her." He sliced off a piece of steak and ate it slowly, savoring every second.

"*Veth*. If the rest of the menu is as good as this, I vote we make this our new home and never leave."

Jaeger bit into his steak and moaned. "I second that vote. Now, we need to hope the club's owners are willing to hire you on as a fighter while I work the gaming tables."

Toro knew what the answer would be, but he made the suggestion anyway. One day, Jaeger would have to face his demons. "You could always sign on as a fighter. You're not as good as me, mind you, but you're not bad."

"Damned by faint praise. I could kick the ass of almost any fighter on the Drift if I wanted to. Present company excluded."

"You should probably include Cynder on that list, too. She'd eat you alive, and not in a fun way."

Jaeger looked back toward the ring, and a ghost of a smile touched his lips. "Yeah, but I can think of worse ways to go. Not that it's going to happen. I've done enough fighting in my life already. I'd rather lug space rocks around then step into the ring. You're stronger than I am, T."

Toro ate in silence. He knew his batch brother carried the weight of every life he had taken while they were soldiers. When they had left service, Jaeger had made a personal vow to never hurt another being ever again. Toro also knew from experience there was nothing he could do to ease his friend's burden. In the years since they had been granted status as human beings and not corporate property, they had both struggled to come to terms with their past while trying to find a future for themselves.

So far, they hadn't been completely successful in either task, but they kept trying. What other choice did they have?

CHAPTER TWO

Cyn was still flying high after her win as she grabbed a quick shower and got dressed. She would celebrate properly later, likely with a few drinks with her brothers and Zura. For now, though, she needed to switch gears back to management mode. She glanced at her watch and swore. She was supposed to meet with a prospective fighter in less than two minutes, and she had left her data tablet with his information in her office. Times like this, she was grateful for her cybernetic implants. She had read the file before, which meant she could simply retrieve the information from her memory banks on her way to the meeting.

"*Veth.* This is what happens when you let yourself get distracted," she scolded herself as she ran a hand through her hair, making the short strands stand up in damp spikes. She took a quick glance at her reflection in the mirror to assess her appearance; it would have to do. Her right cheek was still red and puffy where Frey had managed to land a lucky blow. Twenty minutes ago, it had been bruised, and in another twenty minutes, the microscopic medi-bots she carried in her blood would have it healed completely. Unfortunately, she didn't have twenty minutes. Her meeting was in two—*Fraxx*. More like one minute now. Still, it wasn't like a fighter wasn't going to be distressed over a little bruising. If he was, then he wasn't going to be up to Nova's standards, anyway.

She turned on her heel and left, power-walking the distance from her quarters back to the entrance to the bar. Some days she wished she lived farther away from the noise and mayhem of the club, but there were times the shorter distance came in handy— like when she ran late. Not to mention the fact that every square foot of space in the Drift came at a cost. It was far cheaper for them to live at the club than to pay their corporate landlord even more scrip to live elsewhere.

She re-entered the crowded club without slowing her stride. Her appointment was supposed to meet her at the main bar. She wove through the sea of patrons as she accessed her internal memory drive and scanned it for the pertinent information. She normally tried not to rely on her cybernetic enhancements, but she did make exceptions when they were needed. It wasn't something she made a habit of though. It only served as a reminder to the other races, especially normal humans, that she was different from them.

Her appointment's name was Toro, and he was a cyborg. No surname listed, which wasn't uncommon among her brethren. The corporations that created them officially identified them by the barcode imprinted on their left wrist. Most of them were given names by the lab techs, as names were easier to remember than a string of numbers, but there was no need for last names. She and her brothers, Kit and Luke, had adopted the last name of Armas after they had been freed. According to Luke's research, it meant weapon in one of Earth's ancient languages. It suited them perfectly.

She continued her review, coming up with a photograph of a man who appeared to be in his early thirties with wavy, auburn hair, and dark skin. He was good looking, which was always a bonus. The fans might appreciate talent, but they tended to bet heavier when the fighter was attractive, too.

She approached the bar and spotted Toro immediately. He was as handsome as his picture promised. He stood about six-foot-seven, which made him stand out from most of the other customers. Most, but not all. Standing beside him was another tall, good-looking man with similar coloring and a physique almost as impressive as Toro's. The other man had darker hair and a closely trimmed beard, but they still looked similar enough that Cyn's instincts told her they were likely from the same creation batch. She didn't have anything on the second man, which meant he hadn't put in an application as a fighter. *Interesting.*

They were both watching her approach, and her heart gave an unfamiliar flutter at being the focus of so much male attention. It had been a while since any man had made her heart beat faster.

She walked up to Toro and held out her hand. "You must be Toro. I'm Cynder Armas, one of the Nova Club's owners."

Toro took her hand in his and shook it firmly, holding on a few seconds more than was necessary. When he released her, his thumb caressed the back of her hand. "Nice to meet you, Cynder. I'm Toro, and this is my batch brother, Jaeger. We've been here for a while, enjoying your club."

"Hi there. I'd like to welcome you both to Club Nova. Since you've both had time to look around, what's been your favorite thing so far? The gaming, the tables, the drinks, or maybe the food?"

"It's a toss-up. The steaks were amazing, but I caught your fight earlier. Now, I'd say watching you in the ring beats out everything else," Toro said.

The compliment made her smile and helped to distract her from the lingering memory of his thumb sweeping across her skin. "Thank you. I had a good night tonight. I wouldn't be insulted if you ranked the steak above me, though. It's incredibly good."

"I called Toro a liar when he told me it was on the menu. How are you managing to get real beef all the way out here?" Jaeger asked.

Cyn touched her forefinger to her lips. "Club secret. All I can say is that it's incredibly useful to have your business partners marry a freighter pilot with a lot of connections."

"I imagine it's very useful. As for me, I think my favorite thing so far has been watching how you and your partners run the gaming operations: Good odds, fair payouts, skilled dealers. I'm impressed. Your fight was impressive, too. You do that often?"

"I don't get into the ring often, no. Maybe once every few weeks. I handle the hiring and finances for the club, which means I spend a lot of time at my desk. The fighting gives me a way to blow off a little steam." Cyn inclined her head toward the nearest staff entrance. "If you'd like to come with me, we can discuss things in my office where it's quieter."

"Of course." Toro took the lead, clearing a path through the crowd.

Jaeger gestured for her to follow Toro and fell in behind her, making her the filling in a rather tempting sandwich. Not that she would allow herself to be tempted. For one, she was likely going to offer Toro a contract to fight for the club, which meant for the next month at least, he was technically an employee. There wasn't a hard and fast rule about dating staff members, but it made a handy, and logical, excuse. Then there was the real reason she kept her distance from every man she met: personal preference. She hadn't slept with anyone since being freed from service. Now she had the right to choose, she invariably chose to be alone.

When they reached the door Toro stood aside so she could open it, then both of them followed her out of the noise and crush of the club.

"My office is at the end of the corridor. We should be more comfortable there."

Jaeger stepped through the door, happy to have left the crowd behind for a time. He wanted to see what kind of operation Cynder and her partners ran behind the scenes. What he saw was surprising. Apart from the muffled sounds of the kitchen, things were quiet, and the corridor they'd stepped into was almost empty. A solitary staff member jogged down the hall ahead of them with a keg of beer on one shoulder.

All the doors they passed were clearly labeled, and the halls were clean and clear as far as he could see. He had seen medical centers that were less organized and sanitized than this place.

Toro looked around and whistled low. "Shiny. Not like that last place, right Jaeg? The last place we worked had roaches so big I'm still not sure they weren't deliberately growing them to supplement their meat supply."

Cynder glanced over her shoulder, her face twisted into an expression of disgust.

"That's a horrifying thought. What's the name of the place so I can make sure I never set foot in it?" she asked.

"The Cargo Hold. It's on the Ortan Station near the middle of the Drift," Toro said.

Cynder's lip curled in distaste. "I've been to Ortan. They need to condemn that whole platform and launch it into the nearest star. The last time I was there I saw a bug as big as a dinner plate. It might have been a spider, but the *fraxxing* thing was moving too fast for me to be sure. I don't plan on going back. Ever."

"Not a fan of spiders?" Jaeger asked.

"Not unless I can blast them to atoms. Since Corp-Sec gets bent out of shape whenever someone discharges a firearm, that's not really an option. Me, I would be happy to sacrifice a little hull integrity if it meant killing every eight-legged creature on the Drift." Cynder stopped outside a door with her name on it. "We're here. Come on in."

Once they were inside, Jaeger took a seat and glanced around the office, doing his best to avoid staring at Cynder. He had been trying to ignore the stirrings of interest she aroused in him from the moment he had seen her in the ring, but it was a fight he already knew he was going to lose. She was everything he liked in a woman and then some.

Her short hair showed off the sculpted lines of her face, and her green eyes sparkled with humor.

She had a jagged scar on the right side of her jaw, but it did nothing to detract from her beauty. If anything, it added to the aura of confidence and danger swirling around her. At a few inches over six feet tall, she was average height for a female cyborg, but there was nothing else average about her. Her blue sleeveless top fitted her perfectly, revealing a lean, athletic body with enough curves to make a man take notice.

He was tempted to make a play for her even if she was about to be Toro's de facto boss. It was already obvious to him that Toro was interested. His brother hadn't taken his eyes off Cynder since she had met them at the bar.

The office was a reflection of the woman who worked there. The furnishings were simple; it had minimal decoration and a basic black and gray color scheme. There were several holo-pics on the wall. One showed Cynder and what appeared to be her twin sister standing beside a pair of twinned cyborg men. They were all in standard combat gear, arm-in-arm and laughing. The next picture was of Cynder and the same two men. They were standing in front of the doors of the Nova Club in matching blue shirts with the club's logo emblazoned on them. The men had to be her business partners, but where was her sister?

"How much experience do you have in the ring, Toro?"

Cynder's question brought Yeager's thoughts back to the present.

"I started fighting about six months after we were released from service. It's what I was made for. All my programming and abilities are combat focused. No secondary skills," Toro said with a shrug.

"None?"

Cynder looked surprised, which was understandable. Most cyborgs were created with a primary mission and at least one secondary set of skills and abilities. Toro was an experiment in more ways than one.

"I've picked up a few skills since leaving service, but that's it. Fighting's what I do best."

"Do you like it?" she asked.

That was an interesting question. Jaeger turned to look at his brother, curious to hear what he said.

Toro nodded. "I do. It's not like I get off on hurting people. There's just something about squaring off against another fighter. Testing my limits. Finding out who is stronger or faster. It's a rush." He leaned in and looked directly at Cynder. "I know you know what I'm talking about. I saw it in your eyes when you were in the ring tonight. You feel it, too."

Something flashed in Cynder's green eyes. "The ring is the one place where I'm free to be myself. There's no room for lies. It's all truth. Mine. My opponents. I like that feeling. We might have left the war behind us, but we're always going to be warriors, it's what they designed us to be."

Toro nodded sharply, a big, goofy grin on his face. "You said it better than I ever could, but yeah, that's why I love to fight."

"Normally this is the point where I'd ask about pre-existing medical conditions, injuries, and such. Given that you're a cyborg, I'm betting your medi-bots keep you healthy and fit, so it's a moot point."

"I'm fit. No injuries. I've never even had a hangover."

She chuckled. "That might make you our next star. You're the first cyborg to apply to fight here. I only started doing it a few months ago. In the beginning, we weren't sure how the customers would react." Cynder folded her hands on the desktop and leaned in. "Which brings me to a very important question. Are you willing to do two-on-one fights like the one I fought tonight? It's really the only way to be fair, given what we are."

"Two-on-one is no problem. Unless they're Torski. I've fought a few of those, and they're a fair match one-on-one."

"Considering the males of that species all weighed more than four-hundred pounds and are over seven feet tall, I'd agree with you. No Torski tag-teams. I'll put that in your contract."

"What about other cyborgs? There any chance of you getting in the ring with me, Cynder?" Toro asked, and there was no missing the flirtatious undertone in his words.

She shook her head. "I'd be happy to spar with you, but I'm not sure I ever want to really fight another one of my kind again. You know?"

Jaeger nodded in understanding. For years their kind had been used as pawns in a *bloodless* war between the corporations as they fought for control of resources and territory. Cyborgs were considered products, not people. It was a stance that didn't change until the war ended and the corporations collectively agreed to 'humanely decommission' their remaining soldiers. That was when the entire galaxy learned the truth: the cyborgs had long since overcome their behavioral programming. They were sentient, self-aware beings, and they had no interest in being destroyed. They wanted to be free to live the rest of their lives as they wished. No more wars. No more slavery. No more killing.

"Jaeger's the same way. No fighting our own. Me, I'm okay with it, but only in the ring. Outside the ring, I think we're all sort of a family. Not enough of us left to be fighting among ourselves for real," Toro said.

Cynder glanced over to the holo-pic of her and her twin, and the light in her eyes dimmed. "There aren't nearly enough of us left now."

She closed her eyes, and when she opened them again, she was all business. She looked intently at Toro, then picked up a data tablet and tapped a few quick keystrokes before handing it to him.

"That's our standard contract. I added in the bit about no Torski tag-teams. Look it over and let me know if you have any questions. The short version is that you agree to fight exclusively for the Nova Club for the next thirty days, with an option to renew for another sixty days if we both agree. Payment details are in there, along with potential bonuses. Do you have a place to live yet?"

Toro took the tablet from her. "We've got rooms for tonight, but nothing long term."

"If you want to stay here, we can make occupancy part of the contract, just initial the clause near the bottom about living quarters. We've got space set aside for employees. It's not fancy, but it's cheaper than anything else you'll find. It'll definitely be cleaner than most places," Cynder said and then looked at Jaeger. "The offer goes for you, too. If you're looking for work, we can always use extra bodies around here."

"I suspect we'll take you up on the offer to stay at the club, but I don't need a job. I make my living as a gambler."

Cynder's brows shot up. "Yeah? What games?"

"Only one game, really. Starburst," he said.

She made a wry face. "That game gives me a headache every time I try to play it. Too many nuances to the rules, and I have never figured out how to negotiate the zero-grav zones with the dice. The third time I threw the dice and it hit someone in the head, I took it as a sign to give up. Why not go for something easier?"

He shrugged. "It's the only game I can play without constantly being accused of cheating."

"You mean you get called out less often," Toro grumbled without looking up from the contract he was looking over. "Last place we worked, the bastards took back his winnings even though they admitted they knew there was no way he was cheating."

"That's hardly fair. What did they think you were doing, levitating the *fraxxing* dice with some snazzy cyborg telekinesis power? You won't have to worry about that happening here. You're a cyborg, not a magician. If you can beat the odds and actually win at that damned game, you'll keep your winnings," Cynder said.

"Glad to hear it. To be honest, we came to your club as soon as we heard who owned it. If there's anywhere in the galaxy we could get a fair shake, we figured this would be it." Jaeger said.

"It's better out here than anywhere else I've been. We wandered the cosmos some before finding our way here. I'm betting it was the same for you two," Cynder said.

"Seems to be the story of everyone out here. The Drift is full of souls looking for a new start or a place to hide," Jaeger agreed. The stories changed, but invariably everyone he'd come across was out here because of their past. They were either running from the law, past mistakes, or a combination of both.

"Us included. We're looking for a place to start over," Toro added. He had been listening to the conversation as he worked his way through the contract. It was nearly identical to every other one he had signed since becoming a fighter, though the pay was slightly better and there were benefits, like living quarters and a discount on meals that he had never seen before. It was a good deal, and he planned on taking it. Even if the contract hadn't been ideal, he would've signed it. He liked what he had seen of the club so far, and he wanted to get to know Cynder better. She was tough, beautiful, and probably too damned smart for a grunt like him, but he was going to try his luck anyway.

He set the tablet down on the desk. "How much would it cost to add a room for Jaeger to my contract?"

Cynder shook her head. "It wouldn't cost anything more. We've got space at the moment. If that changes you, two might have to double up, but I doubt it'll happen. We did some renovations and reorganizing a few months ago with an eye to expanding our staff in the future. There's plenty of space."

"You three must be doing pretty well for yourselves to be able to afford all this," Toro commented.

"It was good luck more than anything. Astek Corporation had just taken over this station when we came along. They needed tenants, and we got a good deal on our first lease. We sank every bit of scrip we had left into this place. We were in the red for a year, but business eventually picked up and well, here we are." She gestured around her small office.

She made it sound easy, but Toro knew it had taken more than luck to turn the Nova Club into a profitable business. He and Jaeger had invested most of their settlement money into a startup venture based on holo-vid technology. They'd been promised a rich return on their investment, but less than six months later they had lost most of their money, their pride, and any interest in trusting someone else with their future.

"Any other questions?" she asked.

"Once I sign this, how long until we can move in and get started?" Toro asked, tapping the tablet.

"I did a standard security screening on you before I set up this meeting. Once you sign the contract, you're good to go. Since you'll be living here, too, Jaeger, you'll need to fill out a form so I can run a check on you as well. It won't take more than an hour or so to process. Once that's done, I'll issue you both keycards and club ID."

He picked up the tablet, scrolled to the end of the contract and signed his name, then verified it with a thumbprint scan. "I'm all yours, now."

Cynder chuckled as she took the tablet from him and added her signature and thumbprint to the contract. "Not mine, the club's. My partners wouldn't be happy if I started building myself a harem on company time."

Toro couldn't help himself; he had to ask. "What about building one on your own time?"

"I don't get paid nearly enough to afford a harem. Even if I did, I'm far too busy to enjoy one. If you're looking for that kind of work, though, I do know a few of our female clients who pay very well for uh, personal coaching from our fighters. Want me to let them know you're available for private lessons?"

Jaeger choked back a laugh. "Toro the cyborg gigolo. You know, it has a nice ring to it."

Toro threw up his hands. "*Fraxx*, no. I'm not looking for any kind of private lesson situation. Not my style. The only one I'd be interested in sparring with is you, Cynder. Like I said, I saw your fight tonight. I'd love to take you on someday."

She raised a brow, but didn't say anything for a moment. "I don't know if that will happen, but I've learned never to say never."

Not the willing agreement he was hoping for, but not a total shut down, either. For now, he would call it a win.

"If you don't have any other questions, I'll get Jaeger here to fill out the security check forms and get them started. You two are welcome to hang out at the club until everything is processed and ready," she said.

Jaeger held out his hand for the tablet while Toro shook his head. "No other questions for now.

Thank you for signing me on, Cynder. I think I'm really going to like it here."

She handed the tablet to Jaeger before holding out her hand to Toro. "Welcome to Club Nova's roster. I hope you both like it here."

When he shook her hand, he let his fingers stroke over hers again. She tugged her hand away quickly, but he caught the faint blush staining her cheeks. That subtle change of skin tone was all the encouragement he needed. Boss or not, he was going to keep trying.

Jaeger's voice sounded in his head via their internal comm-channel, his tone one of amused irritation. "*Quit flirting so hard. You're going to strain something. Let's get settled in and form some kind of plan before you go charging in at light-speed.*"

"*Does that mean you're interested, too? I thought you were all work and no play these days?*"

"*I thought you wanted me to loosen up? Now shut up and let me focus on this damned form. The sooner I'm done, the sooner we can grab a drink and come up with some kind of plan.*"

Toro leaned back in his chair and focused his attention back on Cynder. "I think we're going to like it here just fine. Your club has a lot to offer, and I plan on taking it all in. We've been wandering so long I'm looking forward to settling down for a while."

"You wouldn't be the first ones to sign up for a short-term gig and wind up staying. That's why we expanded the staff quarters recently. We keep growing," she replied with a proud smile.

"It's nice to know that our kind can be accepted and successful doing something besides grunt work. I was starting to wonder if it was possible. You should be proud of yourself, Cynder."

She laughed. "I didn't do it alone. You'll meet my partners Kit and Luke soon enough. They're cloned twins with leadership programming. It makes them a little bossy, but you get used to it. They're good guys, so long as you stay far away from their wife, Zura. They're very protective of her."

"I'll make sure to steer clear. She the freighter pilot?"

"Used to be. Now her brother does the flying, and she runs a cargo company. She's easy to spot. Zura's half Pheran and very blue."

"Stay away from the blue woman. Got it." Toro winked at Cynder. "I don't think that will be a problem. As it happens, I've got other plans." Like getting to know Cynder better. A *lot* better. With Jaeger onside, the odds were good. Jaeger was always better at coming up with plans. Toro was too much like his namesake, the bull. He charged in first and thought about things later.

He didn't want to screw things up for them here at the club or with Cynder. He was tired of wandering the galaxy, homeless and alone. They both were. Maybe, if they played their cards right, the Nova Club and its owner could be the answer to all their problems.

CHAPTER THREE

It didn't take long for the two newest additions to settle into the club's routine. Cynder had suspected it would be that way, but when it came to Toro and Jaeger, she was having trouble trusting her instincts. She liked them too damned much to be impartial, a fact that was slowly making her insane.

She wasn't looking for romance. *Veth,* she wasn't even looking for a brief fling. Yet, every time she ran into one or both of them, her pulse kicked up a notch or two, and her thoughts strayed into dangerous territory. There was a reason she didn't date. Several reasons, in fact. She didn't have time for one thing. The club had taken every bit of energy and focus she had while it was getting going. Things were easier now, but it was still a lot of work.

That wasn't the big reason, though. Her true motivation for staying single had nothing to do with the club and everything to do with her past.

Female cyborgs weren't as common as males. The few women that were created were expected to pull double duty, both as soldiers and as sexual partners for their fellow cyborgs. It was part of their behavioral programming, so their compliance was automatic. Even after she and her sister, Dana, learned how to overcome the corporation's control, the charade of obedience had to continue. If anyone suspected that their creations were thinking for themselves, they would have been destroyed. They'd had no choice but to obey orders and stay compliant while they waited for their moment. It had taken years for their time to come.

By the time they were freed, Cynder wanted nothing to do with any man but her batch brothers, Kit and Luke. With Dana gone, they were the only family she had left. They were the exception, though. The only men she let get close to her. Since the day she had been released from service, she had chosen to be alone. Not once had she doubted her choice. Not until Toro and Jaeger came along. The two of them were throwing her well-planned life out of whack.

She caught herself glancing at the security monitors again. "This is getting ridiculous," she muttered to herself.

They hadn't even been here a week yet, and here she sat, mooning around her office and checking the *fraxxing* monitors in hopes of catching a glimpse of either man. She couldn't even put her finger on what it was about them that captured her interest. Well, apart from the obvious fact they were both hotter than a blue giant star. They weren't outright flirting with her anymore; that had stopped after their first meeting. They were friendly when they crossed paths, inviting her to join them for a drink more than once, but when she declined they hadn't pushed her.

She'd kept an eye on them. At first, she told herself it was nothing out of the ordinary. They were new, and she was making sure they were a good fit for the club. After all, they were living there. She quickly learned that Jaeger spent most of his time at the starburst tables, while Toro trained for hours every day. Both of them were damned good at their chosen professions and worked hard to stay that way. Maybe that was part of her interest. It wasn't often she met anyone as driven as she was.

She leaned back in her chair and scoffed at herself. "Or maybe I just need to hook up and get laid instead of overthinking things. Great, now I'm talking to myself, too. It's time to get my head on straight before the guys try telling me I need to go on a vacation or something."

Neither she, nor her brothers had taken any time off since they'd started running the Nova. At least, not until recently, when her partners had taken a well-deserved break to go on their honeymoon. She had managed the club on her own, grateful the staff was second-to-none. It hadn't been easy, but with their help, she had kept everything running smoothly.

Since Kit and Luke's return, they had been encouraging her to take a break from the club. She didn't want to do that. Everything that mattered to her was right here. Why would she leave?

It was clear she wasn't going to get any work done, so Cyn gave up trying. Instead, she turned her attention to the security feeds of the club's main floor. A few quick keystrokes was all it took to fill the far wall of her office with images. If she was going to indulge in a little voyeurism, she might as well go all out. At least this way she was checking in on things around the Nova, which was slightly more productive than she had managed to be for the last hour.

It didn't take long for her to spot Jaeger. He was playing starburst again, and judging by the stack of chips in front of him, he was winning. Again. The dealers all swore he wasn't cheating, which wasn't a surprise given no one knew of any ways to cheat the elaborate game. Cyn didn't think he was cheating, either, but her opinion was based on the man, not the game. She had met more than her share of cheats, hustlers, and con artists in this line of work, and she was certain Jaeger wasn't one of them. He was as smooth as the Keski silk shirts he liked to wear, but his charm had a genuine quality to it, as did the man himself. If he was faking it, he was the best actor she had ever seen.

Her gaze moved from image to image, looking for Toro, but he didn't appear to be in the club. Unlike most of the other fighters, Toro didn't spend all his spare time in the bar. If he wasn't working out or sparring, he was usually in his quarters. For a man made for war, he was remarkably quiet and gentle.

A flurry of movement caught her attention. There was something happening in the gaming section. A tap of a button and she was zoomed in on the problem. *Fraxx.* A couple of human miners were gathered around Jaeger. One of them was angrily pointing to the barcode imprinted on the cyborg's wrist, then to the starburst table. She didn't need to activate the audio feed to guess what the problem was. The idiots were accusing him of cheating because he was a cyborg. Never mind the minor fact that the game was cheat-proof or that Jaeger's cybernetic abilities didn't allow him any advantage over the other players. They were losing and looking for someone to blame.

They were going after Jaeger because he was different from them. That might be allowed in some other clubs, but not here. Not at the Nova. Jaeger might not be an employee. He might not be a friend, either, but he was a cyborg like her, and that made him family of a sort.

She was out of her chair and sprinting for the door a split-second later. Security would likely have it handled by the time she got there, but it didn't matter. She wasn't going to sit here and helplessly watch. This was *her* club, and no one was going to attack a fellow cyborg simply because they were different.

* * * *

Jaeger faced down his accusers with the same icy focus he used to keep himself centered while working with explosives. He had been in this situation often enough that he had learned there was no point in arguing with his accusers. He directed his comments to the dealer, Cassidy, and no one else. "I'm not cheating. I'm on a lucky streak, that's all."

Cassidy nodded, his expression apologetic. "I know," he said in a low tone before lifting his voice and glowering at the ringleader of the troublemakers. "No one is cheating. I need for you and your friends to step away from the other customers, right now. You're holding up play at this table."

"You're taking *its* side?" the largest of the miners asked. He was speaking in Galactic Standard, but his accent was pure Terran.

Why is it the biggest bigots always seem to be from Earth?

The guy was agitated and jittery, unable to keep still. His movements were jerky, his balance was off, and Jaeger noted that the man's pupils were so dilated he could barely see any iris at all. Whatever the miner was on, it had him in a very high orbit.

Cassidy shook his head. "No, sir. I'm not taking sides. I'm enforcing club policy. You and your companions are causing a disturbance and need to leave the gaming area. Now. If you'd like a guide, I'd be happy to call security over and have them escort you."

"I'm not *fraxxing* leaving. I'm a paying customer, and I have every right to be here. I'm not the one cheating!" He pointed a finger at Jaeger. "It's a walking calculator; why is it even allowed inside the club at all?"

Several onlookers took a step back at his outburst, and even some of the miner's friends looked uneasy. Whoever this guy was, he clearly didn't know that the Nova's owners were all cyborgs. Either that, or he was too high to remember, or care.

"That's it, you're out of here," Cassidy said and pressed a small red button on the side of the table. Seconds later, all hell broke loose.

One moment, everyone was standing still; the next Jaeger was ducking a fist aimed straight at his face. He dodged the first blow and then knocked aside the next two without too much trouble. The loudmouth ringleader throwing punches was big, but he was too messed up to for his blows to be fast or accurate. Unfortunately, the bastard also had friends with him, and they weren't interested in waiting their turn. There were three of them attacking Jaeger, and despite his best efforts, some of them were getting past his defenses.

He dodged, deflected, and blocked, but never once did he go on the attack. He had sworn off violence the day he had been released from service. He would defend himself, but that was it. He had no desire to hurt anyone, not even these *fraxxing* idiots. He knew security would arrive any second now and put an end to the fight. All he had to do was keep them busy until then.

The next blow caught him in the upper arm. It was such a light touch it barely registered. Then, the pain started. *Fraxx.* He hadn't been punched at all. He was cut. Hot blood was soaking through the fabric and running down his arm.

"Damn it, I liked this shirt!" he swore as he turned toward the one holding a five-inch blade in his hand. Of course, it was the son of a starbeast who had started this whole mess.

"What do you know? The machine bleeds. I thought you cyborgs were supposed to be tough-ass soldiers. You won't even hit back!"

"If I did, you'd be the one bleeding," Jaeger said.

"Big talk for a cheating machine that can't fi—" was all the other man managed to say before someone stepped in and clocked him hard in the jaw before knocking the knife out of his hand.

The new arrival was Kit Armas, club owner and head of security. He subdued the other two fighters within seconds, leaving only the instigator still on his feet.

"He started it!" the miner bellowed, pointing at Jaeger. "He's cheating. *Fraxxing* cyborg freak."

"You might want to rethink that statement," Jaeger said, not bothering to hide his amusement at the other man's tactical error.

"You have a problem with cyborgs?" Kit asked, folding his arms across his chest and glowering down at the troublemaker.

"Freaks like him should have all been destroyed after the Resource Wars."

"Bryan, shut up!" one of his buddies muttered in Terran. Not that it would help. Jaeger, like all cyborgs, was fluent in every known language in the galaxy.

"Bryan is it?" Kit drawled and pointed to the barcode imprinted on his wrist. "I think you're in the wrong club. In fact, I know you are, because three cyborg *freaks* own the Nova. You've got to the count of five to get out of my club and never come back, asshole. Oh, and Corp-Sec are on their way. If you don't want to deal with them, I suggest you head straight for your ship and get clear of the Drift before the warrant for your arrest goes active."

Cynder appeared beside Kit, her green eyes flashing in anger as she took in the scene in front of her. "You okay?" she asked Jaeger, pointing to his blood-soaked sleeve.

"I'll be fine. My shirt, not so much," he replied. He clamped a hand over the cut on his arm to slow the bleeding. It was deep enough that it would take a few minutes for his medi-bots to clot the blood and begin the healing process. All cyborgs carried variations of the same nanotech. It kept them alive and in fighting form, minimizing their healing time and increasing their odds of surviving wounds that would cripple or kill a normal human being.

Bryan sneered. "Sympathy for a machine? You a freak lover, baby? You can get freaky with me anytime you—"

Cyn hit him hard enough Jaeger could hear the other man's teeth clack together. "Get the hell out of my club. Now!"

"Aw man. You're a machine too? What a *fraxxing* waste of a hot body."

"The only waste here is you. You're a waste of oxygen." Cynder pointed toward the door. "Get out. Your kind isn't welcome here."

For a second, it looked like he was going to be smart and leave. The crowd backed off, and everyone appeared to take a collective breath. That's when it happened. One second, Bryan was standing there calmly, and the next he was lunging for Cynder with yet another blade in his hand and a wild look in his eyes.

"*Fraxx* you, bitch!"

Jaeger charged. He tried to disarm the other man, but the knife wound slowed his response time, and the blow he did manage to land was too weak to knock the blade away. Out of options, Jaeger did the only thing he could; he tackled his opponent and let momentum do the rest of the work. They both landed hard, still fighting.

White-hot pain lanced through his side, and Jaeger deactivated his pain receptors, blocking the pain, for now. Whatever the damage was, his medibots would handle it. Of course, he would heal a hell of a lot faster if he were standing still instead of thrashing around the floor with a bigoted asshole with a knife…but such was life.

He finally managed to wrap his arms around his opponent, pinning his arms to his side and squeezing until Bryan finally stopped moving. The second they were still, Cynder and Kit were there, pulling them apart.

Kit hauled Bryan to his feet and out of Jaeger's field of vision. No doubt to toss his ass out of the club and into Corp-Sec's hands. Rules and laws on the Drift were usually considered more like guidelines, but when blood was spilled, the corporations' private security force got cranky.

"I hate to tell you this, but your shirt's a goner," Cynder deadpanned as she crouched down at his side. "That was a stupid stunt to pull. I'm the fighter, remember? You didn't need to step in, I had him."

Jaeger mustered a grin despite the fact he was still sprawled on the club floor and bleeding. "Do I at least get points for my act of chivalry?"

She scoffed and shook her head. "Yeah, okay. Plus ten for being a dashing knight. Minus several hundred for getting yourself stabbed. Next time you could just open a door for me or something."

"I'll keep that in mind. What are you doing out here, anyway? I thought this was your night off."

"I was trying to catch up on some paperwork in my office. I looked up at the security monitors only to spot a fight going on in the middle of my club with you in the middle of it. I came out to see if anyone needed their head busted, but Kit got here first. Then you tackled that jerk before I could have any fun. Frankly, I'm annoyed at both of you." Cynder tugged up his shirt to look at the stab wound to his side and then pressed her hand against the injury to slow the bleeding.

"Next time I promise not to interfere in your carnage," he said. Despite everything going on, he was acutely aware of her hands on his body. It had been a while since a beautiful woman had put her hands on him, even if it was only to stop him from bleeding on her floor.

"Next time, huh? This happens often?" she asked.

Jaeger shrugged. "Often enough."

"You don't cheat, though. I'm not sure what the *re'veth* you're doing to win at that cursed game, but it's not cheating. My personal theory is that you're some kind of wizard. Maybe you should grow a beard, get yourself a pointy hat and some robes, and make a living doing magic tricks with starburst dice instead. I bet you'd get stabbed less often."

"Hard to say. I'd probably get stabbed a few times for fashion crimes if I wore an outfit like that." Jaeger gestured to his side. "How's it looking?"

Cynder didn't bother lifting her hand to look before answering. "Like you have a hole in your side. I think the bleeding's already starting to slow down. Another few minutes and you'll be good to stand up."

"Then you're going straight to the station's medical center to have that looked at. I'll send Corp-Sec over to take a statement from you there."

Jaeger had to look twice before he could tell if it was Luke or Kit speaking to him. They were cloned twins, and the only way to tell them apart was their hairstyles. Luke wore his a little longer than Kit.

"Hey, Luke. Sorry about the blood on the carpet."

"Why do you think it's a dark color? It hides the blood stains so much better. Does Toro know about this yet, or are you going to let him be surprised when he hears about it through the club grapevine?"

"He's not much for surprises. I was going to tell him as soon as I knew the idiot who did this to me was a safe distance away. The last time this happened, Toro put the guy who attacked me in traction. He's uh, a little short-tempered when it comes to protecting his friends."

Luke glanced at Cyn and grinned. "I wouldn't know anyone like that."

"You're lucky my hands are busy keeping Jaeger's blood inside of his body right now, or I'd kick your ass for that crack. I'm not short-tempered!" Cyn said, glowering at her batch brother.

"Of course you're not. You're a shy, delicate flower. How could I forget?" Luke asked, his eyes gleaming with amusement.

"Hey, mind not riling up my nurse? I'm a wounded man in dire need of her healing touch," Jaeger pointed out, uttering a low, dramatic groan for emphasis.

"Dire need, huh?" Luke raised a dark brow and gave Jaeger a bemused look.

"Not that dire. I think the bleeding has completely stopped now. You ready to get up off the floor?" Cynder asked as she gently eased off the pressure of her hand before finally letting go of him.

"I'd happily stay here a while longer if you promised to put your hand back on my side," he told her, aware he was taking a risk. So far, Cynder had sidestepped every attempt they'd made to get to know her better. This might be his one chance to get past her walls, and he was going to take it.

Luke made a strangled noise as he tried and failed to choke back his laughter, but Jaeger didn't care what Luke thought. The only one whose opinion mattered right now was Cynder.

He didn't breathe again until her lips twitched into a ghost of a smile. "There are easier ways to get to know a girl than getting stabbed in front of her. You know that, right?"

"It seemed like a good idea at the time. Besides, it worked, didn't it? You're here, I'm here, we're talking."

She laughed out loud. "Okay, it worked. I still think it was a little extreme, though. I hope all your romantic endeavors don't wind up with you bleeding."

"They certainly don't start out this way, no. Occasionally they might have ended with bloodshed, but I'm not admitting to anything." Jaeger sat up slowly, keeping an eye on his injury to make sure it didn't start bleeding again. When it didn't reopen, he knew it was time to move, whether he wanted to or not.

He started to get up carefully, and when Cynder offered her hand, he took it. Not that he needed her help. Both injuries were already healing, and he was still blocking the pain, so he wasn't in any discomfort. No, he took her hand because he wasn't a fool. This was progress. If he was going to get past Cynder's armor, he couldn't afford to let chances like this pass by.

"You, get yourself to medical. I know you're already healing, but the doc can take pictures and document your injuries. It will make Corp-Sec's job easier," Luke said.

"Does this doctor know anything about cyborgs?" Jaeger asked as he got to his feet and reluctantly let go of Cynder's hand.

"This one does. She's actually researching us and finding out as much as she can. You might have to put up with a few questions and some annoying pokes and prodding, but she's probably one of the most knowledgeable doctors out there when it comes to cyborgs, and she's not affiliated with any of the corporations."

"I like the sound of that. It would be nice to be able to go to a real doctor instead of back to the lab-techs who designed me the next time I get stabbed, shot, or electrocuted."

Cynder frowned. "Electrocuted, really?"

"Really. I'll tell you all about it on the way to medical."

"Who said I was coming to the medical center with you?" she asked.

It was time to push his luck again. "I'm an injured man, and you're my nurse. You're not going to abandon me now, are you? What if I relapse on the way there?"

Cyn scoffed. "I don't see that happening. You have to be tougher than that, or you'd have never survived the wars."

He wasn't ready to give up yet. "Uh, what if I don't know where the *fraxx* medical is? You can be my nurse and my guide."

"Didn't you download a map of the station when you came onboard?" she asked.

"I didn't. I like wandering around and discovering new places for myself. That's hard to do if I have a map hardwired into my head."

"Fine, I'll walk you to medical. At least that way I can be sure you make it there without getting stabbed again." Cynder took a step and then paused to glower at the curious onlookers in her way. "Move people! Injured man, coming through."

Luke cracked up again. As Jaeger passed him, the other man leaned in and murmured. "You're crazy, but you're getting to her. Keep it up."

"I have no intention of stopping," Jaeger replied.

The moment they were moving, he activated his internal comm channel. *"Hey, Toro. I'm on my way to medical to get checked out. Minor injuries, nothing serious."*

"Re'veth. I'll be right there. Which asshole do I need to maim?"

"Relax. I'm fine. Corp-Sec is dealing with the asshole in question and Cynder is escorting me to medical. Dial down the temper and get down here so we can walk together," Jaeger said.

"Cyn's with you? I'm already on my way. I hope she took the jerk apart."

"Actually, he tried to stab Cynder, so I stepped between them."

"You stepped between…are you kidding me? You're an idiot." Toro was worried enough the last word came out as more of a growl.

"Possibly, but I'm an idiot walking beside a beautiful woman right now. Why aren't you here yet?"

"All right, you're brilliant idiot…and a lunatic. When I said to loosen up a little, this wasn't what I meant. I'll meet you at the front door."

True to his word, Toro caught up to them seconds after they left the club and entered the station's main concourse.

"I can't leave you alone for two hours without you finding trouble. You need a bodyguard, Jaeg. Oh, and I've reactivated the bio-monitoring link between us. I don't like finding out you were in a fight after it's already over."

Cyn snickered. "I never imagined you as the nursemaid type, Toro. Do you tuck him into bed, too?"

"Don't give him any ideas, please," he replied to Cynder before turning his head to greet Toro. "I'm fine. The only reason I'm going to medical at all is because Luke wants a proper report to give to security."

"He really is fine. I checked his wounds myself. This is only a formality."

Toro grunted and fell in at Jaeger's side.

"So, what's the plan?" Toro asked via their comm channel.

"Flirt shamelessly and hope she agrees to go out with us." He hoped that didn't sound as lame as it had in his head.

"Not much of a plan. We tried that already and didn't get anywhere," Toro replied, sounding dubious.

"Luke told me to keep trying. He thinks we're getting to her. I'm taking his advice."

"Did he also tell you to get stabbed? Or was that your own brilliant idea?"

"That wasn't planned. It happened, and I reacted."

"How did you get hurt, anyway?" Toro asked out loud.

"Some idiot accused him of cheating, and they got into it. Kit put a stop to the fight but then the asshole came at me with a knife," Cyn explained as she guided them down the concourse, heading for the central hub of the station. It was approaching the dinner hour, which explained why the place was packed. Residents and visiting crew on leave were all out to find food, drinks, and whatever entertainment they craved.

"Let me guess, Jaeger interfered?" Toro asked Cynder.

"Yep. I'm still not sure if I'm flattered or insulted."

She glanced over at him, and judging by the look in her eyes, she wasn't as insulted as she pretended to be. He was definitely making progress.

"It's the way he is, Cyn. Jaeger would never stand by and watch someone else get hurt if he could stop it."

Cynder stopped and turned around to face them. "Why?"

"Because I've already seen too many good people get hurt or killed. Sometimes, I was the one who did the hurting. I don't want to be that man anymore. I want to be better," Jaeger confessed. He didn't like talking about the past, but he wouldn't lie about it, either. Not to Cynder. If she was interested in them, she deserved to know the truth from the start. They had both done things they weren't proud of during the war.

Her expression softened, and for one brief moment, her guard dropped. Grief, pain, and darkness showed in her beautiful green eyes, only to vanish again a heartbeat later; locked away behind the walls she had built around her heart. "Don't we all."

He knew that look. He had seen it in the mirror too many times not to recognize it. Cynder might have survived the wars, but she had lost part of herself along the way. A strange new thought streaked through his mind, as quick and bright as a shooting star. They were all missing part of themselves. Maybe together, they could find a way to make each other whole again.

CHAPTER FOUR

Toro stayed quiet for the rest of the walk to the medical center. He was too busy watching the interaction between Cynder and Jaeger to talk. Something had changed tonight. It gave him hope that she wasn't as immune to their attempts to know her better as she first appeared. Whatever was going on, he didn't want to charge in and screw it up by saying the wrong thing. Beginnings were delicate things, and he wasn't good at being delicate. He was more of a blunt instrument. Good for bashing and breaking, but when it came to subtlety, he left things to Jaeger. Working with delicate components in high-pressure situations was what his brother was designed for, and he was damned good at it.

The medical center turned out to be only a few minutes' walk from the club. It was nice to know help wasn't far away if something went sideways during a fight. The short walk wasn't short enough to stop them from getting odd looks and outright stares. Jaeger's once-white silk shirt was slashed and bloody, not to mention that Cynder was wearing more than a little of his batch brother's blood on her hands and arms. They were enough of a mess to garner the interest of even the Drift's jaded population.

Once they were through the doors of the medical center, the sights and scents triggered memories Toro preferred not to dwell on. He didn't want to recall the long, dark hours spent in other medical bays and laboratories over the years. The times when he was at the mercy of hard-eyed technicians who treated him and his fellow cyborgs like machines instead of living beings.

"Why do all these places look the same? Just once it would be nice to walk into a medical center that wasn't painted the same damned color of industrial beige," Cynder muttered.

"Better yet, make it a nice, cheerful yellow and make it smell like fresh-baked cookies," Jaeger said.

All three of them laughed, and the dark memories receded again, leaving behind a sense of camaraderie he hadn't felt since the last two surviving members of his batch had left them to seek their fortunes. After that, it had only been he and Jaeger. The two of them against an indifferent and sometimes hostile galaxy.

"What about you, Toro? What would you add to these places to make them more welcoming?" Cynder asked.

"A popcorn machine in the waiting room. You know, one of those old-fashioned ones you only see in vids now. Red and white, with a glass case full of fresh popcorn all drenched in melted butter."

Both of them stopped and turned to stare at him. "I love it," Cynder exclaimed.

"And now I want popcorn smothered in butter. Damn, can you imagine how good this place would smell?"

"You know, I bet we could make something like that work for fight nights," Cynder mused. "I wonder where the *fraxx* we could find a popcorn machine. I'm going to have to ask Zura to put the word out we're looking for one. Her contacts are amazing. If there's one in existence, she'll find it."

The three of them walked up to the reception desk and were greeted by a matronly looking human woman who was all smiles. "You're not on the books for today, Cyn. What brings you by?"

Cynder moved aside and pointed to Jaeger's bloody clothing. "Hi, Anna. We had a situation at the club. Is Dr. Jefferies on duty?"

"As it happens, she is." Anna quirked a brow. "She's with a patient right now. Dr. Basque is free, though."

Cynder shook her head. "Alyson is going to want to meet Jaeger, eventually; it might as well be now."

"Ah, like that, is it?" Anne bobbed her head in understanding and handed Jaeger a data tablet.

"Fill in your information, please. Once you're done, I'll take you to an examination room."

"Where he goes, I go," Toro informed the receptionist.

"Oh, well then, I better put you in the bigger room. The two of you are going to take up a lot of real estate."

"Seriously? I'm already healing. This is just a formality, remember? You do not need to babysit me, T. I'm fine."

Toro crossed his arms over his chest, his jaw set in a stubborn line, and he knew there was no point in arguing. "I want to meet this doctor. She's interested in cyborgs, right? Last time I checked, I was one, too. Odds are one of us is going to wind up back here again, eventually. We might as well get introductions done now."

Cynder snorted. "Fair point. Alyson's going to want to meet you both. In fact, she's probably going to be ticked I didn't introduce you to her already. She's trying to become an expert on what we are and how to treat us."

"Why is that?" Jaeger asked as he tapped away at the tablet in his hand. "Most doctors think we need mechanics, not medical expertise."

Cyn hesitated for a second before answering. "She got involved with us by accident. The story isn't common knowledge, but enough people know about it that you're going to hear a version of it, eventually. You might as well hear the truth from me. A few months ago, Zura was being hassled by an ex-boyfriend. Long story short, this asshole wasn't getting anywhere with Zura, so he kidnapped her brother Royan to get her attention. She, Kit, and Luke went after Royan, and Zura got shot during the rescue. She was close to death with no way to get her to help in time. Kit and Luke took a chance and transferred their medi-bots to her, hoping it would save her life."

Toro blinked in shock. "That should never have worked on a non-cyborg."

"It shouldn't have, but it did. No one knows why. Dr. Jefferies is the one who treated Zura afterward, and she's still keeping a close eye on her in case something changes. Since then, she's become very interested in everything to do with cyborg technology."

"And the corporations are okay with that?" Toro asked, surprised.

"Not really, no. They don't like it, but they can't stop us from going to her. After all, we're not their property anymore."

"Now, I really want to meet this doctor," Jaeger said as he tapped the tablet one last time and then rose to his feet.

"Me, too," Toro agreed.

They were taken into an exam room. It had minimal furnishings: a bed and only a single chair, so Toro claimed an empty corner for himself. He leaned up against the wall, trying to take up as little space as he could. Cynder took the chair, while Jaeger sat on the bed, though he refused to lie down, despite Cynder and Toro's suggesting he do so.

"You're the one who wanted me to come with you to medical as your nurse, remember? So you should be listening to me," Cynder said.

"Well, yeah. But that's because I was hoping you'd hold my hand and whisper sweet, nurturing things to me to keep my spirits up. Not tell me to lie down like I was on death's door," Jaeger joked.

"If you want sweet, then I am not the woman for you."

"Sweet or not, I think you might be," Jaeger said.

"You're flirting, *now*?" she asked.

"This is the first time we've gotten you all to ourselves since our first meeting. So yeah, I'm flirting."

Cynder glanced over at Toro. "Is he always like this when he gets hurt?"

"Never. In fact, he's never like this, period." That wasn't exactly true, but it wasn't the moment to mention that Jaeger was acting like the man he used to be before the years of killing took their toll. These days, he was the only one who saw the old Jaeger; at least, he had been until now. He didn't quite know what else to say, but he felt he had to say something. "We like you and want to get to know you better. You haven't made it easy. So we're here, flirting with you, because now is all we've got."

She stared at him and his gut twisted as he waited for her to say something. Anything.

She rubbed a finger across the scar on her jaw then sighed very softly. "You're serious?"

"Completely," Toro said, not trusting himself to say anything more.

"Then I guess I could give this a shot. I mean, Jaeger did get himself stabbed for me. That's got to be worth something, right?"

"When's your next night off?" Jaeger asked, taking charge.

"Two nights from now."

"Okay. Then two nights from now, we're taking you to dinner. Somewhere outside the club where we can relax and talk and get to know each other."

Cynder nodded. It was tentative, but it was enough. She'd said yes. Toro wanted to cheer. "Thank you,"

"For what?" she asked.

"For giving us a chance." If there was one thing he had learned in his life, it's that chances like this didn't come very often. When they did, the only thing to do was to dig in and hold on.

* * * *

Cynder's head was spinning. How had her evening changed directions so suddenly? One minute she was in her office, mocking herself for watching Toro and Jaeger on the monitors like some pathetic voyeur, and now she had a date with them both. A date. What the hell did she even know about dating? She had never done it. Not once. While she was in service, her encounters with men had been purely physical. A request was made, and she was programmed to comply. There was no romance to it. No flirting or laughter. This was going to be something else, something she had no experience with.

"Save your thanks until after our dinner. By then, you might have regrets." They deserved at least that much warning.

"I doubt that's going to happen," Jaeger said.

"Then you're more of an optimist than I am," she replied. She still wasn't sure why she had opened herself up to them at all. They were attractive, but she never had trouble turning down attractive men before. Maybe it was because they had shown their interest without trying to force things. Maybe it was because Jaeger had gotten hurt in some misguided attempt to protect her. Or maybe she had been alone too damned long. It was probably all of the above, but not necessarily in that order.

Any further conversation was halted by the arrival of the doctor. Alyson Jefferies was a willowy blonde with kind gray eyes and a soft voice that could put even the most agitated patient at ease. Beneath the gentle demeanor, though, was a smart, determined woman who was dedicated to her profession, and her patients.

"Hello. I'm Dr. Jefferies. I understand you were the victim of a knife attack." She offered her hand to Jaeger in greeting.

"Hey, Doc. I'm Jaeger." He took her hand and shook it before continuing. "My shirt's in worse shape than I am. I'm only here because the Nova Club's owners wanted my injuries documented for Corp-Sec."

"Mhmm," she hummed, noncommittally. "Take your shirt off, please. Let's see what the damage is, and then I'll let you know how bad your injuries are. Unless you've gotten a medical degree since you were released from military service, in which case I'll happily take your opinion under advisement."

Toro chuckled. "I like you already, doc. I'm Toro."

The blonde doctor glanced over at Toro, her gray eyes twinkling. "That will likely change once I'm done with your friend and move on to you, Toro. You're both cyborgs, right? I'd like permission to take a few samples, ask you a host of embarrassing questions, and then repeat the whole process from time to time as I come up with new tests."

Toro blinked. "Uh. Really?"

Cynder burst out laughing. "She's not kidding. She's far nicer about it than any of the lab-techs we had to deal with back when we served, though. I promise."

Toro's handsome face folded into a decidedly stubborn frown. "Take a look at Jaeger first, then we'll talk about these tests of yours."

"I think that's the same face you made the first time I broached the topic with you, Cyn. I wasn't serious about doing the tests today. What if we book some time on another day so that we can talk about it? I'll explain what I'd like to test for, and you can decide if that's acceptable to you both. There's a lot I don't know about your kind, and I'd like to remedy that, but I'm not going to push anyone into doing something they don't want done."

"Most cyborgs I've met all had similar experiences when it comes to labs and doctors, but if you're really interested in treating us like patients and not lab experiments, I'm game to come back," Jaeger said. He unbuttoned his bloodstained shirt and eased it off with care, making sure not to reopen either of his injuries.

He looked around for a place to put it, and Cynder held out her hand to take it from him. That was when she finally saw the blood on her hands. Jaeger's blood. Her hands were sticky with it, her forearms smeared and streaked with red. Instantly, she was hurtled into a memory of another time and place. She was lying in the cold gray mud of an unnamed world, her twin cradled in her arms. Dana's blood had covered her then, too. So much blood. Too much. She died as Cynder held her and begged her to hang on. The damage to her body was more than even her medi-bots could fix.

Grief slammed into her, a comet-strike of pain and loss that made her forget everything else. Iron bands locked around her chest, squeezing until her lungs ached, and she had to fight to breathe. The part of her brain still working recognized that she was having a panic attack, but knowing what was happening wasn't the same thing as being able to make it stop. Her heart pounded against her ribs and senses went into overdrive, amplifying everything until she was overwhelmed by it all. The lights flared too bright, the scent of antiseptic and metallic blood made her gag. She scrubbed her hands against her shirt, frantically trying to get the blood off.

Then, someone was behind her. Strong arms wrapped around her, holding her without making her feel confined.

"I've got you, Cynder. Take a breath. Do you need to wash your hands?" Toro's voice was a soft murmur in her ear. He was right behind her, a solid wall of warmth and comfort.

She leaned into him and managed to suck in a lungful of air. "Sink. Please."

He walked her over to the small sink in the examination room, never breaking contact. When she was in front of it, he reached around to turn on the water, filled the palm of one hand with cleanser, and began to gently wash her hands for her.

It was the most intimate thing anyone had ever done for her. Her gratitude at his kindness was mixed with her humiliation at knowing the others had seen her like this. Broken. Useless. Weak. She hated feeling this way. *Fraxx*, she thought was past these stupid attacks. It had been months since the last one. Longer since experiencing one anywhere near this bad.

"Thanks," she murmured, pulling her hands out of his to finish the job herself. She ignored the way her fingers shook as she scrubbed away every trace of blood.

"We've all been there," Toro told her.

He stayed where he was until she turned off the tap, then he gathered up a handful of paper towels and gave them to her before moving away and giving her the space she needed. She dried her hands and inspected them again, making sure there was nothing left to trigger another attack. She didn't want to turn around and face the others. She had no desire to see the looks of pity on their faces, or to see the judgment in their eyes. She knew she was broken, and now, so did everyone else in the room.

She turned around eventually, and her tension eased as soon as she saw that no one was watching her. Jaeger's focus was on the doctor as she ran some kind of scanner over the wound in his side, while Toro was back in his corner, arms across his chest and eyes closed. If it weren't for the lingering nausea and unease she felt, it would be easy to believe her meltdown had never happened. Once again, she owed Jaeger and Toro a debt of gratitude. They were good guys. If they still wanted to go out with her after what they'd witnessed, then she would count herself lucky. Not that she would blame them if they backed out now.

"You're healing nicely. Try not to over-do it for a day or so and you should be back to one-hundred percent. Do us both a favor and try to avoid getting stabbed again for a while, too," Alyson told Jaeger.

"I try to avoid it in general, but tonight things didn't go as planned."

"Mhmm, I hear that from a lot of my patients. I'll write up a report and send it to Corp-Sec. You're free to go. I hope you'll both come back again soon to talk about the tests?"

Jaeger nodded. "I'll be back."

Toro opened his eyes and straightened up to his full six-foot-seven-inches of height, dwarfing everyone else in the room. "Me, too."

"Great! You can organize that with Anne on your way out. Cynder, I'd like to do some bloodwork on you soon, too."

Cynder grimaced. "Didn't we just do that?"

"Mhmm, but I need another sample. I'm working on something new. Please?"

Cyn nodded. "I'll be by in a day or so."

"Make it tomorrow, if you could."

"Okay, doc. Tomorrow." Cynder didn't know what Alyson was working on, but she trusted her. If the doctor wanted her blood, she could have it.

She would do anything to make sure that she and the other cyborgs on Astek Station never had to seek help from the corporate lab techs who had once been their caretakers.

Jaeger got to his feet, and Cyn indulged in a moment of pure, female appreciation for the way he looked shirtless. He was all muscle and strength, with powerful shoulders and a broad chest that appeared bigger now he was out of his clothes. Well, half of his clothes, anyway. The cut on his side was covered, and the stark white of the bandages contrasted with the golden hue of his skin. She glanced away before she was caught staring, but there was no denying he was an attractive man.

Of course, having seen her lose her shit a few minutes ago, he probably wanted nothing to do with her. Why would he? Why would either of them? Doubt gnawed at her insides like a hundred tiny mouths, all of them laughing as they tore into her confidence.

"Give me a second to clean up and we can head back to the club together," Jaeger said, giving her an intent look.

"I should really be getting back. I've still got work to finish and at some point I need to give my statement to Corp-Sec." If they were going to cancel their date, they could do it later, and preferably not in person.

"It's your day off, Cyn. The work can wait, can't it? Walk back with us," Toro said.

She gave a sharp shake of her head. "I'll see you two later. I need to change and clean up properly. Take care of yourselves, and no more fights, okay?"

Toro looked like he was about to argue again, so she didn't give him the chance. She gave a quick wave to Alyson and ducked out the door before any of them could say another word. She didn't want to talk details right now. *Fraxx*, she didn't want to talk at all. She wanted a scalding hot shower, fresh clothes, and some industrial strength mouthwash to get the metallic tang of fear and anxiety out of her mouth.

She barely slowed down as she passed Anne at reception. "I'll be back tomorrow. Doc wants to run some more tests."

Anne didn't have time to do more than nod before Cynder was out the door and back on the main concourse. She spotted two security officers heading to the medical center and breathed a sigh of relief. They had to be here to talk to Jaeger, which meant he would be tied up for a while. She had made good her escape…for now.

Less than thirty seconds later Toro proved her wrong.

"Why aren't you with Jaeger?" she asked as he appeared beside her, his longer stride easily keeping pace with hers.

"He's going to be tied up for a while, so I thought I'd walk you back to the club and grab him a fresh shirt. I'll be back before Corp-Sec's finished with him."

They walked in silence for a little while before she finally spoke. "Back there. I uh…wanted to say thank you for what you did, and for not making a big deal about it."

"It wasn't a big deal. Like I said: We've all been there. We're human, Cynder. We might be stuffed full of tech and enhancements, but we're still human beings. You can't live through what we did and not have it affect you. If it didn't, then the assholes who say we're only machines would be right."

Bitter laughter rose from her throat. "Sometimes, I wish they were right. Don't you?"

Toro shook his head. "No. Machines don't laugh. They don't have friends. They don't care about anyone." He grinned. "They can't appreciate a good cut of rare steak, either."

"Or buttered popcorn?" she asked, smiling a little herself.

"Now you're getting it. We survived, Cyn. I figure that means we owe it to the ones we lost to live the best lives we can. Appreciate everything. Experience all the things they can't. Like going out on a date with a beautiful woman. We're still doing that, aren't we? Going out together?"

"If you two still want to go out with me after my meltdown? Then yeah, our date is still on. I wasn't sure if you'd want to."

"The only reason I'd miss our date is if the universe exploded."

She blew out a breath and her smile grew a little bigger. "Okay then. Toro?"

"Yeah?" he asked.

"I like what you said about experiencing things and living the best lives we can. It's a nice way to think about everything."

"You do?" He looked pleased and a little surprised.

"I do. A lot. Thanks."

"No. Thank you."

She stopped and turned to look at him. "For what?"

"For not laughing."

"Why the *veth* would I laugh at you?" she demanded.

He shrugged. "I'm not good at explaining myself. Not really good at a lot of things, actually. The only thing I know I can do is hurt people. That's it."

His words made her heart ache. She took his hand in hers and squeezed it. "That's not true. You didn't hurt me. You helped."

He closed his hand around hers. "I could never hurt you."

A low, simmering heat started to grow in her heart, slowly spreading outward. She ducked her head as her cheeks started to burn. The man had made her blush. She didn't blush. She didn't hold hands either, but somehow that's what she was doing. Blushing and holding a guy's hand...in the middle of the station's main concourse. *I'm losing my fraxxing mind.*

Toro tightened his grip on her hand and started walking, drawing her along with him. "We should get back, though. You probably want to get changed, and I need to grab Jaeg something to wear. Got anything pink and sparkly in his size? I promise to take pictures if you do."

She laughed. "Do I look like someone who owns anything pink? I could check the lost and found, though. Maybe we'll get lucky."

Toro's rich chuckle sent a tiny thrill down her spine. "Great thinking. Maybe next time he'll think twice before letting himself get stabbed. He's got to start fighting back."

Cyn blinked. "What do you mean?"

"When you get back to your office, replay the security vids. I'll bet my pay for the next two fights that he didn't throw a single punch. He'll defend himself, but he won't fight back. Not ever."

"Never?"

"Not since we left service. Like I said, we've all been there. We all find our own ways to deal with it." Toro gave her hand one last squeeze as they approached the doors to the club, then let her go before they got close enough for anyone to see them. As grateful as she was for his discretion, part of her missed his touch.

"I'll check the vids right after we find him something pink and sparkly to wear." She glanced up at him. "I'm glad you walked back with me."

"I am, too."

This evening hadn't gone at all the way she had expected, but now it was over, she was thankful for every strange second of it. Well, almost every second. If she had it to do over, she would prefer Jaeger hadn't gotten stabbed a second time. Now she knew he wouldn't fight back, she understood why Toro was so protective of his brother. He watched over Jaeger the same way she'd tried to protect her sister, Dana. Toro had done a better job, though. Jaeger was still alive.

CHAPTER FIVE

Toro walked into the small gym and noticed two things straight away. The first was that Dai and Erik, two of the other fighters present, were sporting fresh welts and bruises. The second detail was that Cynder was in the ring, currently matched against the sparring bot they used for practice. She was beating on it with a ferocity that made him worry about the bot's survival. It also told him where the other fighters had gotten their new bruises.

Cynder was on the warpath.

The gym was as well-kept as the rest of the Nova, though the equipment was far from new, and the entire space couldn't accommodate more than a half-dozen people at a time. Instead of investing in a wide array of workout gear, someone had decided to install grav-plates around the space. Workouts could be varied simply by dialing the gravity up or down in your area. It was a slick system, and one Toro had never seen before.

He went through his warm-up routine quickly, keeping an eye on Cynder the whole time. Something was bothering her, and he wanted to know what had changed since last night. Together they'd dug through the lost and found items until they had found a sequined top in a blinding shade of lime-green for Jaeger. She had been laughing as she bid him good night and reminded him to send her pictures later.

She wasn't laughing now.

She knocked the bot into the corner of the practice ring with a vicious kick, and the poor machine started to chatter and chirp in distress as several systems registered damage.

"I think you killed it," he called over to Cynder.

"Piece of junk was half-dead already. I just put it out of its misery."

"You need a new sparring partner?" he offered.

She didn't answer him right away, so he tossed some rocket fuel on her simmering temper. "I promise to go easy on you, sugar."

"Take it easy on me? Oh, you did not just say that. Get your ass in the ring, stud. You're going to eat those words."

Toro joined her in the small practice ring while the other two fighters lugged the dead sparring bot out of the way. Standing this close to Cynder, he could see she was tired. So tired not even her medi-bots could completely remove the dark smudges beneath her eyes or the shadows lurking in her green eyes, dimming their usual fire.

He raised his fists and cocked a brow at her. "You sure you want to do this? It looks like you've been at this for a while."

"She has, and she's leaving a trail of broken bodies behind her. Good *fraxxing* luck, Toro. You're going to need it," Dai stated. He was leaning against a nearby wall, clearly intent on watching the upcoming bout.

"Please, you're not broken. Tenderized, maybe, but you shouldn't have dropped your guard like that."

Dai touched his split lip with his middle finger. "Next time, can you point that out without breaking my face? I have a date tonight!"

Cynder winced. "Sorry. You should have said something. Maybe you should ask her to kiss it better?"

"Good plan. If she slaps me for it, I'm blaming you for that, too."

Toro cleared his throat. "Still waiting to hear if you want to take a break, Cyn."

"I don't need a break," she said and raised her fists.

Toro reached up to tap his knuckles to hers before backing up a few steps. "Then bring it on."

She came at him like a runaway comet, and he had to move fast to block the first set of punches she threw at him. This wasn't the woman he had watched fight in the ring the night they met. Whatever she was dealing with, it had her off her game and running hot. He fought back, matching her blow for blow. She sped up her attacks, and he did the same until both of them were fighting hard and moving faster than any human could hope to match.

"*Re'veth*, if that's what it looks like when they don't hold back, it's no wonder she kicked our asses," Erik said.

"Who said I wasn't holding back?" Toro called over to the spectators.

"You better not be!" Cynder came at him again, but this time, she let her anger get the best of her. Her strikes were wild, missing their target by a few inches each time. She was taking risks, too. Overreaching herself, sacrificing her balance for another chance to hit him. They fought back and forth across the entire ring, neither of them giving any ground at first. He almost cornered her once, but she fought free and then sent him crashing into the ropes with a roundhouse kick that would have caved in his ribs if they weren't reinforced by metal.

He kept moving, drawing her out until she finally gave him the opening he had been waiting for. She attempted a high kick, and he caught her leg as it came around, locking his hands around her ankle and yanking upward. She crashed to the mat with a grunt, and he followed her down, pinning her beneath him.

She swore and thrashed, not willing to concede defeat just yet. He admired her spirit, but he was more worried about the reasons why she was pushing so hard. He managed to catch her wrist in one hand and pinned it above her head as he used his weight advantage to keep her trapped beneath him.

"What's gotten you so grumpy?" he asked in a voice pitched low enough that only she would be able to hear him.

"I'm not grumpy! And *fraxx*, you're heavy! What the hell did they reinforce your bones with, lead?"

"Tungsten alloy, actually."

"Well, that explains it. Hitting you is like punching hull plating," she huffed and shoved at his chest one last time.

"Does this mean we're done scaring the normals?" he asked, inclining his head toward the wall where their audience had been watching.

She looked up then laughed. "They're gone. They probably went to tell my brothers we were killing each other in here."

"So, we can expect them to arrive any second to make sure you're in one piece. That doesn't give us very long for you to tell me why you're beating on your employees and an innocent robot. What happened last night, Cyn? What's wrong?"

She stiffened beneath him, and the light in her eyes dimmed even further. "Nothing happened. I went and watched the security footage like you said, then I had a long, hot shower and went to bed."

Taking advantage of their positions and their brief moment of solitude, Toro lowered his head until their lips were only an inch apart, and he could look deep into her eyes. "Don't lie to me. You can always tell me the truth, Cyn. Always."

"I didn't sleep well. That's all. It was a rough night, and I came down here to work off my stress." Her eyes narrowed. "Happy now?"

"Not really. I don't like seeing you pissed off and hurting." He closed the distance between them and dared to brush a brief kiss to her lips.

She tensed as he kissed her, but once he lifted his head, she relaxed again. "Do, you always take what you want without asking?"

"Not usually. Next time, would you like me to ask?"

"You think there's going to be a next time?" she challenged him.

Toro knew he shouldn't have done it, but he refused to regret what had happened. He had wanted to kiss her since the first time he had laid eyes on her, and even that brief taste of her lips was enough to know he wanted a whole lot more. More kisses. More time in her company. More of everything about her.

He released her wrist and reached down to stroke her cheek, his fingers grazing over the scar on her jaw. It was an angry red this morning, standing out starkly against her fair skin. "I'm hoping there's going to be a next time, yeah. You're amazing. Why the hell would I want to stop at one kiss? You're sexy, tough, funny, and you throw a mean left hook. I've never met anyone like you before."

"I've never met someone like you, either. No one else is crazy enough to try to kiss me while he's got me pinned to a mat. Then again, it's been a few years since anyone managed to pin me at all, so you also have that going for you." She closed her eyes and added. "Next time, I'd appreciate it if you asked me first."

"Cyn, may I kiss you before I let you up?" he asked.

She cracked open an eye and laughed. "You don't waste any time, do you? Okay, crazy man, one kiss."

This time, he didn't stop with a gentle touch. He cupped her cheek in his hand and slanted a heated kiss across her lips. Fire streaked through him when she lifted her hand and tangled her fingers in his hair, tugging him closer. His cock hardened in seconds, and there was nothing he could do to hide his reaction from her, not when they were plastered together from chest to boots. She tasted like sugar-dusted berries, sweet and ripe with promise and he knew one taste was never going to be enough.

Cynder's eyes flew open, and she uttered a frustrated groan. "Up. We need to get up, now! We're about to have very concerned company."

Toro's thoughts were so tangled it took him a second to figure out what she was talking about, and by the time he understood, it was too late to move.

"What the hell is happening?" One of the twins bellowed as footfalls pounded toward the gym.

"Are you okay, Cynd—" The door was flung open so hard it nearly came off its hinges, and Luke charged through the door, coming up short when he spotted his sister and Toro tangled up on the mats.

"I ran down here to make sure you two were still in one piece and this is…not what I expected to find. Damn it, warn a man, will you? I don't need to see this!" Luke said, averting his eyes to the ceiling.

"Sorry," Toro muttered as he pushed himself off Cynder.

"Not your fault. You did have permission after all," she said, then turned to her batch brothers, who were both now standing in the doorway with stunned expressions. "Don't you dare say one word, either of you. Utter a single syllable and I'll bring up every time I walked in on you two and Zura, starting with that time I found you having sexy breakfast time on the counter and working in chronological order up to that incident last week where I found you three in the fight ring…"

Kit threw up his hand. "You made your point. So, uh, any reason why Erik was pounding on the office door claiming the two of you were beating the hell out of each other?"

"We weren't beating the hell out of each other. We were just practicing. I was in a bad mood, and after I broke the sparring bot, Toro offered to spar with me. I guess we got a little out of hand and panicked the normals."

"You broke the bot? Again? Those things are *fraxxing* expensive, Cyn!" Luke exclaimed.

"Erik was concerned enough that he sent us both down here to make sure you both survived whatever the hell you were doing, so yeah, I'd say you panicked them."

"It's been a while since I went all out with someone I knew wasn't going to wind up hurt if I did. I guess I got a little carried away," Cynder said.

"*We* got carried away. It was fun, though. I'm game to do that again any time you want. Though maybe next time we should warn everyone else to stay clear, yeah?" Toro got to his feet and then offered a hand to Cynder, helping her up.

"That would be a good idea." Kit frowned. "So uh, you two are good?"

"Really? You need to ask that? Out, you big jerks. Both of you."

Luke snickered. "If you hadn't deactivated our internal comm channel, this wouldn't have happened, so don't get all cranky with us. Be glad we used to be your commanders and still have broadcast override or you wouldn't have known we were coming at all. I shudder to think what I might have walked in on if that had happened."

"Strawberry pancakes and whipped cream, Luke. Health violations in the club's commercial kitchen. Remember?"

Luke's mouth closed with an audible snap.

"I'll track down Erik and Dai and apologize for letting things get out of hand," Toro said. "For the record, you never have to worry about Cynder when she's with me or Jaeger. We'd never hurt her."

"Not even if they tried," Cyn added.

Kit stared at Toro for a long time, then nodded. "If you ever do, you better be off the station and clear of the Drift before Luke or I find out about it."

"Out!" Cyn yelled, blushing wildly. "You want to go all protective and alpha, do it with your wife. She thinks it's cute. I don't."

Cynder waited until her brothers had left the gym before turning to Toro. "That was an interesting end to our sparring session."

He ran a hand through his hair and gave her a look hot enough that she felt like she'd fallen into a star. "Any time you want to *spar* again, you just let me know. Maybe next time we'll do it without an audience, or interruptions."

"Not even Jaeger?" she asked. She still wasn't sure how she felt about whatever this was evolving between the three of them, but if this was happening, she needed to know what she was getting herself into. Due to the way they trained and fought, most cyborgs were tightly bonded to at least one other person in their batch. It was obvious that Toro and Jaeger had that connection. Cyborgs bonded that way tended to share everything, including their romantic partners. She was pretty sure they were looking to share a woman, but before this went any further, she wanted to be sure.

"If Jaeger was with us, he wouldn't be part of the audience. He'd be a participant. At least, that's what we're hoping for. That's your call, though, not ours."

She liked that he had given the choice over to her. She liked it a lot, actually. "I agreed to go to dinner with both of you, didn't I? I only wanted to be sure. Things like this, they can get complicated if everyone isn't on the same page. Not that we have a thing, exactly."

He cocked his head. "I think we might. Have a thing, that is."

"One kiss doesn't mean anything," she stated.

He hauled her into his arms and held her tight, his head bowed until they were so close that their breath mingled.

"That kiss meant something to me, Cyn. *You* mean something to me. I'm not good at finding the right things to say, but I wanted you to know that."

Fraxx. He was sexy on a bad day, but when he said things like that and looked at her like she was the center of his world, her entire body hummed with need and her heart pounded like she had done a ten-mile run in double gravity. "I think you said that perfectly."

He actually blushed a little at her compliment, and her libido slammed into hyper-drive. Who knew the big, sexy, brute had a bashful side? It was completely unfair.

"Before I let you go, are you sure you don't want to tell me why you were in such a lousy mood this morning? I know there's more to it than you've told me."

She didn't want to talk about it. It would only show him how broken she truly was, and that wasn't how Cyn wanted either of them to think of her. "Does it matter? I feel better now."

"Nothing like beating up two guys and a robot to put you in a better mood?"

"They weren't what helped. That was all you."

He actually blushed again. "I'm glad. The next time the nightmares come, message me. We'll meet down here, and I'll give you a repeat performance."

"Who said I had nightmares?" she asked. For someone who kept saying he had no gift for anything but violence, Toro was damned perceptive.

"You did. You're tired this morning, and I know that look in your eyes. I've seen it in Jaeger's often enough and mine, too."

She blew out a breath and leaned into his chest, just a little. "Okay, I had some bad dreams. Seeing Jaeger bleeding yesterday, the blood on my hands, it made me remember something I don't like to think about."

"Is that when you got this?" he asked, stroking his thumb over her scar.

"Yeah. Do I want to know how you figured that out? I thought Jaeger was the magician, does that make you the mind-reader?"

He chuckled. "I pay attention to things. For one thing, we don't usually scar. The medi-bots make sure that doesn't happen. So however you got this, it was bad enough that you couldn't heal yourself properly. This morning it looks irritated. Like maybe you've been rubbing it."

"You're smarter than you give yourself credit for. I got this the night my twin sister died. Her name was Dana. She was..." Her throat tightened, nearly choking off her next words. "She was the best of us all. I should have protected her better. I should have saved her somehow."

Toro tucked her head beneath his chin and held her close. It was the first time in her life anyone had made her feel small, like something delicate that needed to be cherished and protected.

"If she was your twin, then I imagine she was amazing. Just like you. We were at war, Cyn. You can't blame yourself for what happened. I bet she wouldn't want you to, either."

"She was my rock. The only one who could keep me grounded. Life without her is...less."

"You lost your twin. Life isn't ever going to be the same, but maybe, it shouldn't be less of a life. You know?"

"My head knows that, but my heart still hurts. It's easier when I don't think about her or any of it."

"Then Jaeger got himself stabbed and you were right back there again?"

"Pretty much. Only this time the outcome was a lot better. How's he doing?"

"He's fine. If he follows that doctor's advice and takes it easy today, by tomorrow, it'll be like it never happened. The only real casualty is his shirt. He's still whining about that."

"He's got good taste in clothes. Every time I see him he's dressed to kill, and I don't think he's worn the same thing twice," she said, eager to change the subject to something besides her sister and the past.

Toro snorted with laughter. "It's nice to know you've been paying that much attention. Jaeg likes his clothes all right. The day we were released, he went out and spent a lot of scrip on new outfits. Tailored. Nice fabrics. Nothing like the uniforms we used to wear."

"Well, we can add the cost of a new shirt to Bryan's tab. That bastard still owes us for his drinks last night. He might as well pay for the shirt, too. After all, he's the one who ruined it."

"I'm glad that's all he ruined. You know, if he hadn't lost his mind, you and I wouldn't be here right now. I'm a little grateful to the asshole."

She burst out laughing. "That's one way to think about it. I don't think Jaeger would share your gratitude, though."

"I don't know about that. We've got a date with the most beautiful woman on the Drift tomorrow night because of what happened. I think that's worth a little pain and bloodshed. I'm betting he would, too."

"You're only saying that because he's the one who bled."

Toro loosened his hold on her just enough to be able to lean back and look at her. "No, I'm not. Jaeger's the only friend I have in the whole *fraxxing* galaxy. I never want to see him hurt. Back when we served, part of my duty was to protect him. I've been watching his back since the day we started training. That's never going to change."

"The rest of your batch is gone?" she asked, then frowned. "Whoa, hold up. You were assigned to protect Jaeger?"

He nodded, and his next words were steeped in sadness. "Most of them are gone. There were only four us left by the time we were released. Ward and Vic are cloned twins, commanders, like your partners. We lost touch with each other a while back. Last I heard, they were heading out to the Drift. They're one of the reasons we ended up out here. Maybe we'll run across them one day. They're the only family we've got left."

"If you stick around here, I bet you'll find them. Every ship working the asteroid field comes into the Drift, eventually. That's only the answer to my first question, though. What about the second?

Why were you assigned to protect Jaeger? He seems perfectly capable of taking care of himself."

"Jaeger was our demolitions expert. Building and defusing explosives. For him to do his job, he has to be totally focused on what he's doing, or we all went boom."

"Dangerous work. He was lucky to have you."

Toro snorted. "I saved his ass more times than I can count, but the truth is, he saved me, too. I was created to be a straight up killer. They only gave me one skill set: the ability to hurt my own kind over and over for no other reason except those were my orders. Sometimes, it felt like keeping him alive was the one good thing I *could* do. It was the only thing that made me human instead of a killing machine."

Cynder reached up to twine her arms around Toro's neck and leaned back to at him. "You're not a machine. None of us are. You reminded me of that last night. We're more than that, Toro. You're a man, and I think you're a good one."

His lips curved into a slow smile. "Thank you. It means a lot that you'd say that. Jaeger and me, we've traveled all over since we left service. We've seen a lot of places and met a lot of people, but none of them were our friends, and no place felt like home. Not until we came here and found the Nova Club. This place is different."

Pride swelled inside her. "That's what we always wanted this place to be. Not just a club, but a home."

"I think you've succeeded. Maybe, if things work out, Jaeger and I can make it our home, too. I mean one day, not today. We should probably go on our first date before I start talking about the future, huh?" He leaned down and pressed a kiss to her cheek before losing his hold on her.

"A date might be a good place to start," she said, releasing her arms from around his neck and taking a step back. She needed space to think about what had happened between them, and what might happen tomorrow night. She also had to figure out how she was going to deal with her batch brothers and their teasing, because she knew damned well there was going to be a lot of it. They were going to enjoy getting back at her for all the mockery and laughter she sent their way when they had fallen for Zura.

Veth. Their payback was going to be a bitch.

"Tomorrow night feels a long way off," Toro grumbled. "Maybe we can meet up for drinks tonight?"

She shook her head. "It's fight night. I'm going to be busy and so are you, if you want to be. You're not scheduled to fight, but we could use you out on the floor as security personnel. You interested?"

He grinned. "Cracking heads on the outside of the ring instead of inside? Count me in."

"Great. I'll tell Kit. He'll get you a uniform and tell you what you'll need to know. Basically, be polite, be firm, and when they don't listen, try not to hurt them too badly."

Toro nodded. "I can do that."

"I know you can. I wouldn't have asked you, otherwise." Cynder hadn't planned to ask Toro to help. It wasn't something they did often, because most of their fighters didn't have the temperament for security work. They were more likely to pick fights then stop them from happening.

Toro was different than the others. He didn't have anything to prove. *Fraxx*, based on what she was seeing, he could probably take down every fighter they had without breaking a sweat. Even when she came at him too hard, he hadn't gotten angry, and the moment he took her to the mat the fight had ended. If things went well tonight, maybe she could offer him a different career path than the one he was on. One with a future that didn't require him stepping into the ring every week for the rest of his life. He deserved more than that.

Now, she had to explain to Kit why she had taken it upon herself to hire extra security for tonight and what she was hoping it would lead to. He would laugh at her and tell her she was going soft, but she was fairly certain he would bring Toro onboard for a shift and see how he did. They never talked about it, but the Nova wasn't just their home. They'd created it with the intention of making it a place any cyborg would feel welcome. The one place in a cold, indifferent, galaxy that anyone like them could find a place where they belonged.

"I'll see you later," Toro said. "And Cyn? Thanks. For everything."

"Anytime, and next time, you're going down."

He grinned at her. "Until next time, then."

She headed to her quarters for a quick shower and tried to ignore the thrill that chased down her spine every time she thought about being back in the ring with Toro, or better yet, back in his arms. The man could kiss even better than he could fight, and for her, the combination was as sexy as hell.

CHAPTER SIX

Meetings were far from Jaeger's favorite way of passing the time, and meetings with security personnel were even further down the list. Yet, here he was, having a meeting with Corp-Sec for the second time in twenty-four hours. At least they had been polite about it. They had contacted him on his comm device and asked when he could meet with them instead of ordering him to appear. They even offered to meet him at the club, an offer he was happy to take them up on. It was the first time local law enforcement had treated him decently. The moment the Corp-Sec officers entered the room, he understood why. They were cyborgs.

Both of them were dressed in the deep red uniforms of corporate security, the closest thing the Drift had to a police department. They kept the peace, enforced the rules when needed, and generally saw to it that the denizens of the Drift didn't plunge the entire place into perpetual chaos.

The officers weren't alone, either. Kit Armas was close behind them, followed by Luke and Cynder. Cynder did a double take when she saw him sitting there, then blushed slightly as she made her way to an empty chair to his right.

"Hey, Jaeger. I didn't know you were going to be included in this briefing," Luke said as he grabbed a chair from the table.

"I was told to show up by Corp-Sec, so here I am. This is a briefing?" Jaeger asked, arching a brow at Kit. Kit knew he would be here; he was the one who gave him directions to the room.

"I thought that's what it was. Mack, what's going on?" Cynder asked, looking at the cyborg security officer with black hair. His partner was a blond, and they showed none of the usual similarities that would mark them as batch siblings.

"We figured we might as well have you all in at once to tell you what's going on with the investigation. Save us repeating ourselves. Kit knew about it; I don't know why he didn't tell the rest of you."

Cynder glowered at her brother. "I have a pretty good idea. Not even a little bit funny, Kit."

Kit guffawed. "Oh, yeah, it was. I wanted to see your face when you saw the other one, and now I know everything I need to."

"Asshole," Cynder muttered under her breath.

Now it made sense. Kit wanted to see how she reacted to his presence after catching her with Toro this morning. His brother had told him all about their sparring match, the kiss, and getting caught by her brothers. The big man hadn't been able to shut up since he got back from the gym. It was the happiest Jaeger had ever seen him. Judging by Cynder's blush when she spotted him, she was as affected by the morning as his batch brother. The only way he could be happier right now, was if he had been the one to kiss Cyn instead of Toro. That was something he hoped to rectify shortly.

"I don't know what any of this is about, and frankly, I don't want to know. That way when the inevitable sibling smackdown happens, I have deniability," the blond Corp-Sec officer stated as he took the last seat at the table, the one directly across from Jaeger. "I'm Officer Dash Scudo, by the way, and this is my partner, Officer Mack Darian. Nice to meet another fellow veteran of the wars."

"Jaeger. Nice to meet you, too, I think. Unless you're here to arrest me. If that's the case, it's going to put a damper on a budding friendship."

Mack snickered. "You, I like. As it happens, we're not here to arrest anyone, but there are a few things you all need to hear about the fight last night and what caused it...and why our suspect isn't going to be charged with anything."

"What?" Cyn slammed her hand down on the table. "Why the *fraxx* not? He tried to stab me and he managed to stab Jaeger, twice!"

Dash ran a hand through his short blond hair and sighed. "Cool your rockets, Cynder. We're not charging him because he's dead. Not a lot of point in charging a dead man with anything."

Veth. "How did he die?" Jaeger asked, hoping like hell the fight last night hadn't left Bryan fatally injured somehow. He didn't want any more blood on his hands.

"Overdose. At least, that's the coroner's preliminary assessment. The initial arrest report noted he appeared to be on something. He was out of his mind by the time they got him to headquarters. Extremely violent and ranting incoherently. They put him in a cell to calm down, and an hour later, he dropped dead. No warning. No nothing."

"What the hell causes that to happen?" Kit asked.

"*Crimson,*" both officers answered at the same time.

"And what the *fraxx* is *crimson*?" Cyn asked.

"It's a new drug that appeared on the Drift a few months ago. It's a bright red liquid sold in small ampules. A few drops under the tongue is all it takes. It's not licensed, so none of the registered pharma dealers are supposed to touch it. It keeps showing up, though, and we haven't been able to figure out who is bringing it in or how."

Luke curled his lip in obvious distaste. "Come on, guys, don't lie to us. It's the Drojo Cartel, isn't it?"

Jaeger winced. He had heard of that cartel. They were a nasty crew of pharma traffickers so mercenary they'd sell their own sisters if it made them a profit. He wasn't aware they were this far out, though. "Don't they usually stick closer to Earth controlled territory? What the hell are they doing way out here?"

"They're expanding their operations. Their goal is to take complete control of the illegal pharma trade for the entire Drift. We caught a few low and mid-level operatives the time they kidnapped Zura's brother, but we haven't learned anything to lead us to the ringleaders or tell us where their base of operations is."

Kit growled in frustration. "If any of them set foot in the club, they're dead. I don't care if they've broken any laws or not."

"We know. Which is why we're having this meeting. After what they did to Zura and her brother, Corp-Sec is willing to look the other way if they cross your path, but only to a point. This new pharma is nasty stuff. In small doses, it's just another psychotropic, but take too much, or take it too often, and wham, the user goes into what they're calling red-rage. Totally out of control, violent, and dangerous to everyone around them. Until now, only a handful have gone full rager, but that's changing. In the last three days, we've seen eight cases of red-rage. Of those eight, three are dead, and two are in medical with uncertain outlooks. We need information, so try not to kill anyone who might be able to help us shut their operation down for good," Mack said.

"I'm not making any promises," Kit said.

"If they come near our wife or her brother, they won't live long enough to be helpful to you. Sorry, Mack, but there's no way we're taking that kind of risk."

Jaeger wanted to know more about what happened to Zura and her brother, but even more than that, he wanted to know why he was involved in this meeting. He could have been told about Bryan's death in a simple message. There had to be some other reason he was here, and he said so. "What exactly does this have to do with me?"

"You're in the Nova every day, but you're not part of the staff. You might see things others wouldn't. If you do, we're hoping you'd give us a heads-up," Dash explained.

"You want me to spy for you? Do I get a codename? If I'm going to risk getting stabbed again, I should at least get a cool codename." He already knew he would do it. It was the right thing to do. If Bryan's actions were anything to go by, this new pharma was dangerous, and apparently, the Drojo Cartel had a history with the owners of the Nova, which meant Cynder could be in the line of fire. If he could help keep her and her family safe, he would do it, even if she wouldn't appreciate the sentiment.

"How about Stabby?" Luke suggested.

"Pincushion?" Kit said, barely able to control his laughter.

"You're both hilarious. You ever consider having a comedy night at the club?" Jaeger asked, leaning back in his chair.

"Codename aside, is that a yes?" Mack asked, pointedly ignoring everyone else.

"If it makes the Nova a safer place, then yeah, I'm in. Do you want me to let Kit know if I see anything, or tell you directly, or both?"

"Both," Kit said before anyone else could speak. "I'm the head of security, if something's going on, I need to know about it. Your guys were slow arriving last night. If there's more trouble, I'm not going to wait on Corp-Sec before dealing with it. Your job is to protect the whole Drift. Mine is simpler. I only have to defend what's mine."

Dash raised a hand. "Don't blow a circuit, Kit. You hear about a problem, you deal with it, same as always." He turned to Jaeger. "We'll trade contact info with you before we leave. If you see anything suspicious, let us know…right after you tell Kit," he amended quickly.

"You got it. And uh, convey my thanks to the two Corp-Sec guys you sent to interview me last night. That's the first time in a long time I've actually been treated like a victim and not another suspect."

Mack nodded. "Most of our guys have learned not to judge cyborgs without having the facts in hand, first. It helps when their bosses have barcodes, too." He tapped the black imprint on his wrist.

The meeting broke up not long after that. He exchanged contact information with Mack and Dash, as well as Luke, Kit, and Cynder.

"For use only in emergencies, or do I have permission to contact you even if I don't see criminal activity?" he asked as he entered her code into his comm device.

Her lips quirked into a faint smile. "Use your best judgment."

"I'll try, but it can get mind-numbingly boring staring at a starburst table for hours on end. Talking to you would help pass the time."

"I've got a job to do, remember, and now, so do you, Diceman." She grinned. "I've decided that's your codename, by the way."

"Diceman, huh? Apt."

"I thought so, too. It looks like both of you got new jobs today. Do you two do anything separately?"

Jaeger leaned in close. "We're a team. I hope someday soon you give us an opportunity to show you how well we work together."

The tip of her tongue stroked over her lower lip, and all the blood in his body rushed straight to his cock.

"Keep asking nicely and maybe you'll get your wish someday."

"I'll do that," he managed to say, but it wasn't easy to form words when all he could think about was how much he wanted to kiss her. It wasn't just her body that made him want her. It was her brain.

She was smart as hell, funny, and tough enough to fight through the darkness he had caught a glimpse of yesterday at the medical center. He knew why she wanted them to ask permission, too. He couldn't blame her for wanting that small courtesy. Not after what she and the other female cyborgs had lived through.

She was worthy of his respect and consideration, and he had no problem demonstrating that any way she wanted them to.

Cynder knew her brothers were watching the two of them, and she didn't like it. They needed to get over this protective big-brother routine at light speed. Her life was her own, and she could spend her time with anyone she wanted to. She didn't need their approval, and she certainly didn't want them shadowing her like overzealous chaperones.

"Walk me to my office," she said to Jaeger. "On the way, you can tell me where we're going for dinner tomorrow night."

"The location's a surprise. It's a little spot I found while I was exploring the station." He offered her his arm in a gallant, old-fashioned gesture that made her smile. Especially when she caught Kit glowering at them.

"Is it going to be crowded? Should I dress up? Give a girl a hint." She kept up the light banter as they passed her siblings and started down the corridor to her office.

Jaeger raised his voice slightly— just enough to be sure their audience heard every word. "No crowds. In fact, we'll be the only ones there. I'm hoping that will give us a chance to get better acquainted without any interruptions."

They kept walking, and as soon as they were out of earshot, Jaeger chuckled. "That was fun. Am I going to pay for that later?"

She shook her head as she grinned. "Nope. I'm going to call in the big guns. Zura will make them behave themselves. She might look sweet, but she's got a core of steel."

"Really? She's always so soft spoken."

"Then you haven't seen her mad. She can curse a blue streak, pun totally intended. She's all big silver eyes, sweet smiles, and cute blue blushes until something sets her off. Once her fuse is lit, it's best to take cover."

"But she's half Pheran. They're a pretty mellow species, aren't they? Especially the females."

"Her mother was Pheran, but she was raised by her dad. He was a freighter jockey and a smuggler. Believe me, she's as tough as they come. Not long after my brothers finally decided to make their move, a nasty piece of work named Vin Collins came back into her life. He was the ex-boyfriend I told you about, an abusive son of a starbeast who wanted her ship."

"I can't imagine that went over well with your brothers."

Cynder snorted. "Not at all. That's how this whole mess with the Drojo Cartel started. Vin worked for them. When Zura wouldn't play ball with him, he kidnapped her half-brother to force her hand. She and my brothers went after them with Corp-Sec as back up. Vin ended up dead, along with a lot of low-level cartel members. For a while, we thought that would be the end of them out here. Looks like they're back again."

"So who killed this Vin guy? Zura?"

"Kit. Zura was busy rescuing her brother at the time. That's when she got hurt and ended up with the medi-bot transfusion. One of the cartel bastards shot her."

Jaeger blew out a breath. "You people don't live quiet lives, do you?"

"Where would the fun be in that?" she asked.

"You sound like Toro."

"Is that a bad thing?"

"No, but it does explain why you and he get on so well," he said.

Cynder considered that for a moment, then stopped walking and turned to face him. "That doesn't explain why you and I get along, though."

"I don't know why that is, exactly. I don't know you well enough yet." He leaned as if he were going to kiss her, but stopped a few inches away. "I'm looking forward to figuring it out."

"You and me both, Diceman. Can I maybe have a clue as to what I should wear? Is this a high heels or combat boots situation?"

"No heels unless you want to wear them. This isn't a high-end establishment we're going to, but I promise, the atmosphere is amazing. Dress in whatever you're comfortable in. We'll be at the door of your quarters at six to escort you to dinner."

"I can meet you two there, you don't need to come get me."

"Yes, we do. For one thing, you don't know where we're going, and for another, it's good manners for us to meet you and take you out. I've been reading up on this."

"You have?" she asked.

Jaeger actually looked a little sheepish. "We haven't done this before. Not a real date. I wanted to do it right."

With that confession, Cynder fell a little more under the spell Jaeger and Toro were casting. "I haven't done this either. I guess that's something else we can figure out together."

"I'm going to ask you for permission to kiss you now, Cynder," he murmured, moving another half an inch closer.

"Permission granted. But if either one of my brothers sees us, they're going to be a pain in the ass about it."

"I'll take the risk." He closed the final distance between them and kissed her, drawing her into his arms at the same time.

He smelled good, a subtle musk that made her want to fill her lungs with his scent. His mouth covered hers in a slow, seductive kiss that built with every passing second. His beard rasped against her skin, tickling her just a little as their mouths mated, and the heat between them grew ever hotter.

She wrapped her arms around his waist and held him close, enjoying the way his hard body pressed against hers. He kissed her for another moment then lifted his head to stare down at her, his light brown eyes gleaming with desire.

"That was worth any risk," he murmured.

"I think so, too."

He released her then and escorted her to the door of her office. "I'll see you tonight. I know you're going to be busy, but I'll be around. If you've got a free minute, join me for a drink?"

"If there's any time, I will," she said, surprising herself. Usually, she wouldn't make time for anyone or anything on a fight night, even one she wasn't scheduled to be in the ring for. Ever since they had married Zura, Kit and Luke had been at her to take more time for herself. Maybe it was time she took their advice. Even if it did mean listening to them gloat about it later.

Jaeger ran his knuckles down her cheek. "Until later, then, beautiful."

She managed to make it into her office with the door shut before she let herself indulge in a long, happy sigh. Getting involved with Toro and Jaeger was still a bad idea, but *veth*, it sure felt good.

CHAPTER SEVEN

Cynder couldn't sit still. She had already changed her outfit twice and swapped shoes three times, and now she was prowling her quarters while her sister-in-law watched in open amusement.

"This is a new look for you," Zura commented from her spot on Cynder's sofa.

"What is?" She glanced down at the outfit she and Zura had finally agreed she would wear on her date. "What are you talking about, Little Blue? I've worn this before."

Zura laughed and tipped her head to one side before giving her a sideways smirk. "Not the clothes, the attitude. I don't think I've ever seen you nervous before."

"I'm not nervous. I'm a *fraxxing* war veteran who fights in the ring for fun. I don't do nervous."

"Really? Because you're pacing so much you're making me dizzy, and I bet you've clocked nearly a mile in those shoes since you put them on. If you're not nervous, then you should probably cut back on your caffeine intake."

"You're a pain in the ass. You know that, right? Why did my brothers marry you again?"

"Because you helped them see I was the right pain in the ass for them. Something I will always be grateful for. Now, I'm returning the favor. Jaeger and Toro seem like good guys. I'm glad you're giving them a chance."

"We'll see. I'm still not convinced this is a good idea, but…" Cyn shrugged then dropped onto the couch beside Zura. "I wanted to say thanks for coming over to help me decide what to wear. I was making myself crazy. This isn't something I have any experience with, you know?"

"I know." Zura leaned in and bumped their shoulders together. "If your brothers can figure this out, so can you."

"I sure as *veth* hope so. Nothing against your husbands, but I'm the *smart* one in this family."

Zura snickered. "I know. Don't tell them I said that, though. Luke is certain it's him."

"Not even on his best day." The moment of shared laughter took the edge off her ragged nerves, but only just. A quick glance at her watch told her there were still ten minutes to go before her dates would arrive. There had been ten minutes the last time she looked at her watch, too. Maybe the damned thing was broken? She gave her wrist an irritated shake, but the time remained the same.

"If I have to sit here, waiting for another second, I might explode," she muttered.

"Then don't wait. If they wanted a sweet, meek woman they'd be having dinner with someone else tonight." Zura pointed to the door with a grin. "Go get 'em."

"I'm gone. Thanks again, Blue."

"Anytime. Have fun and don't do anything I wouldn't do!" Zura called out, still laughing.

"I'm not making any promises," she called back as she left her quarters and made her way to Toro and Jaeger's rooms. She hadn't seen much of either man since the day before, and she was eager to change that. Fight night had been busier than normal, so she'd barely had time to say more than a brief hello to Jaeger last night. That many people meant security was a challenge, too. Cyn was happy Toro had been there to lend a hand. He didn't have to do much; one look at the towering cyborg dressed in the club's uniform was enough to keep most of the patrons in line.

The uniform looked good on him, too. The dark blue, sleeveless shirt clung to him like a second skin and showed off his powerful arms and swarthy skin tone. She wasn't the only one who had been admiring him, either, and that irritated her more than she expected it would. Logically, she knew one kiss didn't give her any right to get all possessive about either one of them, but her heart did not agree.

Her heart rate jumped as she neared her destination. *This is only dinner; it doesn't mean anything*, she reminded herself. She stopped outside their doors and pondered her next move. Lurk in the hallway and wait for them, or knock and announce her arrival. If she knocked, whose door did she go to? All three of them were going to dinner, but she could only knock on one door at a time. She didn't want to look like she was picking one of them over the other.

"How the *fraxx* does Zura do this?" she muttered. Still uncertain how to proceed, she decided to double-check her outfit. Instead of her usual blue and silver uniform, she wore a dark green skirt that fell to mid-calf and a simple, black, scoop-necked top. She tugged on one sleeve, took a breath, and threw up her hands.

"Eenie-Meenie-Miney-Mo, catch a comet by the—"

She stopped when she heard Jaeger's voice coming from Toro's room. "…No, I'm not imagining it, asshole. I'm telling you I heard Cynder."

The door opened, and Jaeger leaned up against the jamb, a grin on his face. "Hello, beautiful. I thought we were supposed to be coming by to get you, not the other way around."

"I was ready early and didn't feel like waiting. Is there a reason you're in Toro's room and not across the hall in your own place?"

"I was early too, so I wandered over. Unlike Toro, I know how to tell time." He glanced over his shoulder and called out. "Hey, T. Cynder's here. You're now the only reason we're not already on our date, so move your ass."

"*Fraxx*! She's early. Gimme a minute."

Something crashed to the floor, and she heard Toro cursing in three different languages. "He okay?" she asked.

"He's fine. Just running a little late." Jaeger's gaze roamed over her, his eyes gleaming with approval. "You look fantastic."

"So do you. New shirt?" He was wearing black slacks that fit him to perfection and a dark blue shirt that looked soft enough to stroke. Whatever the fabric was, she hadn't seen it before, which meant it likely wasn't cheap.

"I spent some of my winnings and picked up a few things. Staying here has freed up a bit of scrip I would have otherwise needed to spend on rent. Thanks for that."

"You're welcome. It's really no big deal, though. We have space right now; you might as well use it."

"It is a big deal. You took a chance on us, and I'm not going to forget that. You and your partners are building a good thing here. I'm glad to be part of it."

"Is that why you agreed to be Corp-Sec's eyes and ears?" she asked.

"In part, yeah." Jaeger stood up straight and offered her his hand. "It might also be that I don't like the idea of anyone threatening you, your family, or your home. I know you can take care of yourself, but I like the idea of being able to help. If what we saw last night is any indication, this new pharma is going to be a problem. I'd rather it wasn't a problem for the Nova or my friends."

She took his hand, lacing her fingers with his. "Anyone ever tell you that you have a serious nobility streak, Dice?"

"Nope. This is a recent development." He raised her hand to his lips and brushed a kiss over her fingers. "It started the second I met you."

Her brain melted a little around the edges, and her stomach filled with butterflies at his words. She even blushed a little to complete her body's betrayal. It was impossible to look aloof and in control with pink cheeks and a goofy smile plastered on her face, so she stopped trying. "Do I get to know where we're going, yet?"

"Down," was his cryptic reply.

"Down is not a location, it's a direction. And given that this station doesn't have gravity, it's not even an accurate direction at that. Down is whatever way the grav plates say it is."

"It might not be a location, but it's all you're getting. We'll be there soon. We'd be on our way already if Toro had mastered the art of dressing himself." He winked at her and turned around.

"Do you need a hand, T? Remember, pants on before your shoes."

"So much for nobility," she teased him as he turned to face her once again.

Jaeger shrugged. "He's my brother, he doesn't get the noble treatment. I've seen you with Luke and Kit, so I know you're exactly the same way."

"Yeah, I am. Family are the ones you can abuse, and they love you anyway."

"Exactly."

Toro appeared at the door a few seconds later, and it was all Cyn could do not to stare. He barely resembled the shirtless fighter who had taken her to the mat only two days before. His auburn hair was pulled back into a ponytail for one thing, and he had ditched his usual casual outfits for a pair of black leather pants and a crisp white shirt with a V-neck that showed a teasing hint of broad chest and muscle. He had donned a black leather vest to finish the outfit, and as far as she was concerned, he looked incredible.

"Sorry to have kept you waiting, Cyn. It took me longer than I expected to make myself look presentable. I'm out of practice."

"It's fine, Toro. You're not late; I was early. By the way, you don't look presentable; you look great. Both of you do." She held out her free hand to Toro and smiled. "I'm a lucky woman."

"I think we're the lucky ones," Toro replied, tugging her hand until she moved in closer to him. "You take my breath away."

"I'll be right back. I need to grab our dinner, then we can get going." Jaeger released her hand and squeezed past Toro, back into the room.

"We're taking dinner with us?" she asked.

"No food dispensers where we're going," Toro said.

"You're not going to give me a hint, either?"

"Not even a little one. You're just going to have to trust us."

Jaeger reappeared and handed a backpack to Toro. "You take this, and I've got the rest."

"Got it." Toro slung the bag over his shoulder while keeping hold of her hand. Jaeger reclaimed her other hand, and the three of them started walking down the corridor. A quick glance told her that Jaeger was carrying another pack the same size as the first. She was more than a little curious to know what was in them.

When they reached the doors to the club's main floor, Jaeger squeezed her hand. "If you'd like us to let go of you now, we will, but we don't want to. I want to walk out there and let everyone see the beauty we're taking to dinner."

"Same here. You're with us, and I want everyone to know it, but only if you're okay with it."

"Who said I was letting go of either of you? If I didn't want anyone to know about this, I wouldn't have said yes in the first place. Besides, if anyone says anything, Toro can deck them and afterward I'll ban them from my club."

"Sounds good to me," Toro said and opened the door.

It was early enough the club was still relatively quiet, but they garnered a few curious looks as they made their exit.

They were only a few feet from the door when Kit's voice boomed out from the far end of the club. "Have her home by ten, boys, and keep your hands to yourselves!"

Laughter and rowdy applause filled the bar. "I'm going to kill him for that," Cyn muttered, half tempted to turn back and lay into her brother here and now.

"Revenge is a dish best served cold. C'mon, beautiful. We'll plot their demise over dinner," Jaeger said.

"Or I could hurt them now if you'd rather. Your choice," Toro added, making her laugh.

It was nice to have them both ready to defend her, even if their methods varied. "Dinner and demise, I think. I'd rather be with the two of you than spending any more time on my idiot sibling."

"Your wish is our command, milady," Jaeger said. He led them out of the club and across the main concourse to a maintenance door she had never noticed before. He pressed his palm to the scanner, and seconds later, the door opened.

"Do I want to know how you did that?" she asked.

"I told you, I like to explore. I used to build and dismantle bombs for a living, remember? Rewiring a simple scanner was easy, and it gives me access to the more interesting parts of the station."

"Illegal access," she pointed out, following him through the doorway. "If our date ends with us getting busted for trespassing, I may never speak to you again."

"We won't. No one's going to disturb us. I have a plan."

Toro groaned. "Every time you say that, it all goes to hell. What's the plan, Jaeg?"

"You mean he didn't tell you, either?" Cynder asked.

"Not everything," Toro replied. He directed a frown over Cynder's head toward his brother. He wasn't sure what Jaeger was up to, but the lack of information was worrying their date, and that wasn't okay with him.

"Enough with the secrets, Jaeg. Tell her what we're doing down here before she gets mad and walks away." He sent the message via their internal channel.

"On it," Jaeger sent back and then started speaking out loud. "We have permission to be here tonight. I talked to your friends in Corp-Sec after our meeting yesterday. Since they didn't come through with a codename for me, I asked them to get me access to the lower levels instead. There's nothing down there but maintenance corridors and support equipment, so they said yes...eventually."

"Codename?" Toro asked. He had already heard about the meeting and what Jaeger had agreed to, but there had been no mention of a codename until now.

"He wanted one for being a Corp-Sec spy, and I've given him one. He's Diceman, Dice for short."

"You asked for a codename? There are times I worry about you, Jaeg. Did they drop you on your head when they pulled you out of your maturation tank? Maybe you should go back to see that doctor again and get your head checked."

"Did you see Dr. Jefferies today?" Cynder asked.

"Yeah, we both did. I got a clean bill of health, and we let her do the tests she wanted," Jaeger said.

"You were right about her. She's different than the corporate lab techs. She was gentle and explained everything she was doing. It was nice to be treated like a person and not a lab experiment." Toro was impressed with the doctor. Not only had she treated them decently, but she seemed committed to finding out more about how they were made and how best to treat them.

"Yeah, she's one of the good ones," Cynder agreed.

"Did you go back to see her yet, or have things too busy around the club?" he asked.

"I went yesterday. She's noticed there were some differences in the bloodwork between the male and female cyborgs on the Drift and wanted to do more tests."

"How many female cyborgs are there around here? I've only ever met one, you." Jaeger asked.

"According to the doc, there's three of us. Me, one in Corp-Sec, and the other's a miner between contracts. It wasn't until the miner came in that Alyson had enough samples to notice there were differences. She didn't say what kind; she just said it wasn't anything life-threatening. Comforting, huh?"

Toro felt a band of iron tighten around his chest at the thought of something being wrong with Cynder. "She'd tell you if it was important, wouldn't she?"

Cyn nodded. "Of course she would. She's doing this because she cares. The corporations that created us aren't too happy about her interest, either. She told me several of them have been in contact, trying to discourage her from continuing her studies. They're claiming they still have a proprietary interest in the technologies used to make us."

"That's bullshit. We're free citizens. If she has our permission to run tests, that's none of their *fraxxing* business," Jaeger protested.

"That's pretty much what she told them, too. It makes me wonder what they don't want her to know. It's not like she's going to build a cyborg army of her own. Even if she had the means, it's a moot point given that the entire practice is illegal everywhere in the known worlds."

There had been a lot of disagreement, blame sharing, and denial from every government and agency about the cyborg program, but all of them had agreed on two things: the cyborgs were free-willed beings, not property, and the technology to create them should never be used again. The corporations had fought the rulings, but in the end, they had been forced to comply. Instead of terminating the lives of their former soldiers, the companies who had created them were required to not only free them, but they had to pay them for their time in service.

Jaeger led them to an elevator, and the three of them rode in silence as it took them down to the lowest levels of the station. When the doors opened on the bottom floor, Cynder laughed and glanced at Jaeger. "Down, huh?"

"I told you that's where we were going."

"You did. I didn't expect you meant it quite so literally. Where are we, anyway?"

"You'll see in a few minutes; we're nearly there."

Toro looked around with curiosity. He hadn't been down here before, and this part of the station was laid out differently than the sections he had seen. There were two identical corridors leading to the left and right. There were no obvious signs indicating what lay in either direction, just a pair of arrows with an indecipherable set of letters and numbers beside them. The corridors were more like tubes. The "floor" was only discernable because it was marked by a double set of pale green glow-strips. The air was several degrees warmer, and there was a trace of condensation on the curved metal walls.

They went to the left, and after less than a minute, Toro felt a disturbing disconnect between what he saw and what his other senses were telling him. Cynder slowed, too, and they exchanged a look between them.

"Grav plates?" she asked.

"I think so. Would explain the round hallway."

Jaeger glanced back. "Sorry, forgot to warn you about that. This part of the station doesn't maintain a constant gravity field. This tunnel lets us reorient to a different horizon. Compared to where we started, we're about halfway up what was left-hand wall."

"You could have just said the grav plates are making us walk on the wall," Toro grumbled.

"If I'm too queasy to eat dinner, I'm going to be grumpy. This feels weird," Cynder said.

"You've waged battle on countless planets, survived hundreds of high orbit dropship entries, and you're complaining about a little gravity disruption?" Jaeger teased.

"I guess I'm going soft. Civilian life is making me into a delicate flower."

Toro scoffed. "Not even a little bit, sugar. You're still a sexy-as-hell hardass."

She beamed. "You say the nicest things to me."

"And that right there proves that you are truly the woman for us. If he tried that line on any other woman, she'd be insulted or in tears by now." Jaeger stopped outside another locked door. "We're here."

He passed his hand over another scanner, and the door slid open. Warm air flowed around them, carrying the scent of green, growing things. It had been so long since he stepped foot on a planet, Toro had almost forgotten what it was like to breathe something other than recycled air.

"What in the worlds?" Cynder's voice was tinged with wonder as she peered past the doorway to the wonderland beyond.

The door opened out onto a landing near the bottom of a sphere more than fifty feet across. The walls were lined with row after row of brackets, all of them full of plants bathed in constant light from the hundreds of lamps shining down on them from a few feet above the tallest leaves. The brackets were divided into sections by marked pathways, and a catwalk spanned the midsection of the sphere, linking to of the main paths.

Jaeger gestured for Cynder to enter the sphere. "Welcome to Astek Station's atmospheric farm, or as I've decided to call it, the atrium."

"I had no idea this place existed. I've seen the outside of the station plenty of times, and I've never seen any sign this is here at all. How did I miss it?" Cynder stepped over the threshold, then turned and beckoned them to join her inside, her face wreathed in smiles.

"I wondered about that myself, so I looked up the plans for these stations. It turns out that only half of it is visible from the outside." He pointed over their heads. "That portion appears as a hemisphere at the bottom of the station. The part we're standing on is inside, out of sight."

Toro groaned. "We're standing upside-down right now? Is that why we were walking on the wall earlier?"

"They do some funky things with the gravity down here. I get it; they can use more of the space this way, but only away from the inhabited areas."

"I can't believe they still use organics as part of the oxygenation process. No one does that anymore, do they?" Cynder wandered over to the edge of the landing and ran a gentle hand along the leaves of one of the plants. "I'd forgotten how pretty greenery could be."

"This station is older than it looks. The system still works, so I guess no one's bothered to modernize it." Jaeger pointed to a section of plants that looked different from the others. "I think that's a herb garden, and on the other side I found some flowering plants I suspect are what they sell at the florist shops on the station."

"I always wondered how they managed to get fresh flowers this far out. My brothers will cry when I tell them they've been spending a fortune on posies that were grown under their feet instead of on a planet."

"I doubt it. If flowers make Zura happy, I bet Luke and Kit would pay any price. They clearly love their wife and would do whatever it took to please her," Toro said.

"You got that right. She could probably ask for a moon of her own, and they'd try to get it for her. Lucky for all of us, Zura's not that kind of woman. If she was, the club might be bankrupt by now."

Toro crossed the landing to stand behind her, trapping her between himself and the plants she was caressing. "What would it take to please you, Cyn? What would make you happy?"

She glanced back over her shoulder and smiled at him. "I'm a simple girl. I don't need flowers, or moons, or presents of any kind. I don't take time for myself very often. My brothers would say I don't take it at all. Spending time with the two of you is making me happy. No club. No worries about unlicensed pharma, or security, or balancing the books. More of this would make me very happy."

"We can do that. All I need for you to make me happy right now is for you to tell me I can kiss you again."

"Yes."

He wrapped his arm around her waist and pulled her up against him, relishing the way her body melded to his. She leaned into him with a soft, contented sigh, and he gave in to his need to kiss her. He hadn't been able to steal another kiss since their bout in the gym the day before, and it felt like forever since he tasted her lips.

She tasted like cinnamon tonight, hot and sweet and sinful. Need tore through him, sending his pulse racing as his cock grew instantly hard. *Fraxx*, all it took was a touch, and he was on fire for her. Whatever was starting between them, Toro already knew it was more than lust and physical attraction. This was something that could alter his life's orbit forever if he let it. Standing here with Cynder in his arms and his brother at his back, Toro couldn't think of a single reason to resist what was happening. Out of all the futures he had imagined for himself and Jaeger, none of them compared to the reality that was Cynder Armas.

CHAPTER EIGHT

Cynder lived to take risks. She was always the first one to rush into battle, the first to hop the fence or throw herself into the next adventure. There was only one part of her life that she guarded, one thing she never took chances with: her heart. After all the death she had witnessed and all the dark grief still locked inside her, she had never taken a chance and let herself get close to anyone. Not until Zura had joined their family and Cyn had found another sister, not a replacement for Dana, but someone new to care for.

Zura's arrival had caused Cynder to lower the walls she had built, and now Toro and Jaeger were in her life, threatening to make their own claims on her heart. Letting them in was a gamble, one she wasn't sure her already battered heart could survive.

"You're thinking too much, Cyn. Stop thinking and just be." Toro's words surprised her, and she peeked up to find him smiling down at her.

"I know that look," he explained with a shrug. "Jaeger gets it when he's calculating outcomes and worrying about variables while life passes him by."

"New rule. No bashing the other guy and keeping our date all to yourself at the same time," Jaeger said, appearing beside them.

"I don't like that rule; I'm choosing to ignore it," Toro replied before kissing her again.

This time, his mouth branded hers, taking no quarter as he kissed her with breathtaking intensity. Her heart hammered against her ribs, and she strained on her toes to reach up for him, eager for more. Toro was right. She had played it safe long enough. It was time to be true to who she really was. It was time to take chances again.

He groaned in approval when she moved to meet him, and his arm loosened from around her waist just long enough to turn her around to face him fully. He crushed her against the hard planes of his chest as his tongue slipped past her lips to dance with hers. By the time he broke their kiss, she was panting softly, her heart was pounding, and her legs were trembling slightly.

He released her without a word, and before she could speak Cynder was wrapped in a second pair of arms and pulled into another scorching hot embrace. Jaeger's kiss was explosive, his mouth claiming hers with a fiery passion that ignited her blood and made her pussy slick and wet. Sparks of desire sizzled along every nerve as the needs she had denied for ages came surging to life in an all-consuming firestorm.

"I've been waiting to do that since yesterday," he whispered against her mouth when they finally slowed for a moment. "Tell me I won't have to wait that long to kiss you again."

"No more waiting," she replied. "No more asking for permission. My answer will always be yes."

Jaeger's light brown eyes darkened with regret. "I'm sorry. I forgot to ask that time, didn't I?"

"You did, but that's okay. Toro remembered, and I was hardly going to tell him yes and you no. We're in this together, all three of us, right?"

"All three of us," Jaeger agreed.

Cynder wrapped her arms around Jaeger's shoulders and leaned in to nuzzle her lips against the side of his throat. "Thank you for bringing me here. I had no idea there was beauty like this anywhere on the station."

"It's lovely here, but if you want to see beauty, Cyn, all you need to do is look in a mirror."

She shook her head. "When I look in the mirror, all I see is the sister I lost."

He was silent for a moment, but his arms tightened around her in silent support. "One day, I hope you'll tell me about her."

"One day," she agreed.

"But not tonight," Toro interrupted, his tone gentle. "Tonight is about laughter, good times, and lots of food. Speaking of food. Eventually, you're going to have to let go of her, Jaeg. Otherwise, we're never going to eat."

"To paraphrase someone I know, I don't like that thought, so I'm choosing to ignore it."

She laughed at both of them. "You might want to ignore it, but I don't. I haven't eaten for hours, and I'm hungry. Food first. Play time second. There's no need to rush, is there? The night is young, and there's nowhere else I'd rather be."

Struck with a thought, Cynder pulled her comm-device out of her pocket and held it out to Jaeger. "I'm not going to need this tonight. Why don't you keep it for me? I'm officially unavailable until our date ends."

Jaeger took the device and slipped it into a pocket. "It would be my pleasure."

He kissed her one last time, a tender brush of the lips that left her aching for more. Before she could react, he released her and moved away. He grabbed the bag left lying on the floor and opened it, rummaging through the contents until he found what he was looking for.

A thick, red blanket appeared first. He tossed it to Toro, who spread it out on the floor of the landing. She watched as the two of them quickly set up an entire picnic, complete with chilled bottles of beer, a loaf of thickly sliced bread, an array of cold cuts and cheeses, and even condiments in squeeze bottles. When Toro opened the last container, her mouth watered at the aroma wafting out of it.

"Is that fried chicken?" she asked.

"It is. Zura might have mentioned it was your favorite," Jaeger said. He indicated the feast with a courtly flourish. "Milady's repast awaits."

"This looks great. I'll admit I was wondering what you were planning on serving considering where we are." She sat down cross-legged and reached for the nearest bottle of beer. When she saw the label, she groaned. "This happens to be my favorite beer, too. Zura again?"

Toro scratched the back of his neck, his lips twisted into a sheepish grin. "She wanted to help. She uh, gave us a list."

Veth. "A list? What list? When?" Cyn asked. She wasn't sure if she was more amused or mortified that Zura was so involved in her social life. She was going to have to have a word with her little blue sister-in-law.

"She walked up to me while I was working security two nights ago. We chatted briefly about my new gig, then she handed me a handwritten list and told me to read it," Toro said.

Cyn twisted the top off her beer and took a long drink before speaking again. "Do I want to know what was on it, or would that information put her life in danger?"

Jaeger chuckled and shook his head. "It was just a few suggestions about what you liked. Food, drinks, your favorite color, stuff like that. She also added a note to the effect that if we upset you in any way, she knew more than a dozen places to hide our bodies where they'd never be found. For a Pheran, your sister-in-law is remarkably bloodthirsty."

"You have no idea," she retorted before taking another sip of her drink.

"I know enough to be sure I never want to be on that woman's bad side. Your family is a little scary, Cyn." Jaeger settled on the blanket to her right, and a moment later, Toro sat down on her left.

"We look out for each other. You know how that is."

Toro nodded. "We do. It's been us against the rest of the galaxy for a long time now. That's why I like it at your club. Everyone who works here seems cool with who and what we are. It's nice."

"It wasn't like that in the beginning, but over time, we found the right people for the job, or in some cases, they found us." She raised her bottle in a toast. "To finding the right people. I'm glad the two of you came to the Nova. The club is better for having you here."

The three of them toasted with their drinks and then started to pass around the food as they talked about everything from the other fighters at the club to their adventures since being freed from service. The only topic they left alone was their time spent as soldiers. This wasn't the time for reliving the darkness of the past. Tonight was about making new memories.

There was another reason they didn't discuss the Resource Wars. It was something of an unwritten rule among the cyborgs not to mention which corporation had created them, or which side they had fought for. Most of them had been enemies at one point, and it was easier not to know if you'd ever faced someone you knew in battle. Some things were better left unknown. Now the war was over, they were all the same. They were survivors.

* * * *

The more time Jaeger spent in Cynder's company, the more certain he was that she was the piece that had been missing from their lives. After they'd left military service, he and Toro had tried dating, both together and separately. They'd quickly learned that dating separately wasn't the right choice for them. They had spent too many years together and experienced too much to ever live completely separate lives. The women they dated invariably ended up jealous or angry over the bond the two men shared. It was far better to date the same woman. If they could find one both of them desired, and who was interested in becoming part of a triad. Cynder was everything they had hoped to find, and so much more besides.

When they finished their meal, the three of them worked together to clear everything away and return it to the bags for the trip back home. Not that they were going anywhere yet. He had another surprise planned for tonight. One he hoped she enjoyed as much as the picnic.

"Anyone want another drink?" Cyn asked.

"Not for me," Toro said.

"I'm good for now. I thought it might be a good time to unveil the next part of the evening's entertainment," Jaeger replied.

"There's more?" she asked.

"Our conversation about popcorn the other day got me thinking. How does popcorn and a vid sound? I've got a couple loaded onto my tablet to choose from, and Toro tracked down popcorn. I don't know how, but he did."

"It's not hot, but it was made today. It seems you can find almost anything on the Drift if you ask the right people." Toro said.

"It sounds perfect, what vids did you pick? Please tell me Zura's list didn't include movie choices."

"No such intel was provided. I checked. Which is why we have a selection. Lady's choice." He picked up the tablet he had pulled out earlier and handed it to her, stealing a kiss at the same time.

"My choice? Let me see..." She scrolled through the options and quickly made her selection. "Oh, you got the remake of *The A-Team* vid on here! Let's watch that one."

"I have all three remakes, actually. Which one's your favorite?" he asked.

Cynder blinked. "There are three? How did I miss one?"

She started reading more closely, and after a minute or two, she tapped in her selection and handed him the tablet. "I had no idea they made one back in the early twenty-first century. Where did you even find a copy?"

"We were on an ancient relic of a freighter for one leg of our journey out here. The vid was in the entertainment computer's database. I got permission to copy it before we left the ship."

"This is going to be good. Thank you both so much. I'm really having a great time tonight."

Toro got to his feet and offered a hand to Cynder. "Time to get to our seats for the movie, up you get, sugar."

She gave him a perplexed look. "I'm already sitting."

"Trust us, the view is better where we're going."

Jaeger had filled Toro in on the rest of his plan during dinner. It would be a little tricky, but between the two of them, they would manage.

Cynder took Toro's hand and allowed him to help her to her feet. She didn't protest when he kept hold of her hand and tugged her into his arms for a kiss that nearly set the air around them ablaze. Jaeger's mind immediately started thinking of everything the three of them could be doing soon, and he completely forgot about the vid projection he was supposed to be setting up for a few minutes. It wasn't until Toro nudged him with his boot that Jaeger snapped out of it.

"Vid, Jaeg. In order for us to enjoy the vid, you actually have to play it."

"Right. Working on it." He kept the tablet placed so it was blocking Cyn's view of his lap and his rock-hard erection. All he had to do was think about her and his cock sprang to life. He didn't plan on rushing into anything, but his dick was keen to push their relationship to the next level at light-speed.

"Where are these seats you spoke of?"

"Up," Jaeger responded, well aware he was baiting her.

"Again with the vagueness, Dice. Are we going back to the Club?"

"We're staying in the atrium." He pointed toward the catwalk. "Up, in this case, means that way."

"You haven't let me down so far, so I am going to assume there's a plan once we get up there."

"Yep. C'mon, I'll show you something else I discovered when I was reading up about this place."

The three of them took one of the pathways leading to the catwalk. He led them out to the middle of it and rifled through the bag he brought with them. It didn't take long to find what he needed. It was a length of rope twenty feet long. He tied one end to the railing and fastened the other end to the bag. Now came the part he wasn't sure about. According to his research, he needed to be standing exactly dead center in the middle of the catwalk for this to work.

"Here goes nothing," he said and tossed the bag straight up into the air. It soared over their heads and stayed there. *Perfect.*

"Zero-g?" Cyn asked, her eyes still on the floating bag. "I was going to ask how, but I think I've figured it out. The grav plates all have a maximum range of influence, and this is a perfect sphere. To stop the grav plates from interfering with each other, there would need to a buffer zone, where there's no gravity at all."

"Nothing sexier than a smart woman. The buffer zone is about fifteen feet across, which is plenty of room for the three of us. One zero-g movie theater, ready when you are."

"How do we get up there? If you think you're tossing me up there like the bag, you can forget it."

Toro laughed. "I'd like to see that."

"Dream on, stud. That's never going to happen. Can we jump?"

Jaeger nodded. "The effect should start ten feet up. Make sure you grab the bag or the rope, though. You'll be moving fast enough to drift out of the bubble."

With a whoop of joy, Cynder launched herself upward. She hit the edge of the zero-g bubble and started to tumble, but she managed to grab the rope and stabilize herself quickly enough. Her skill wasn't a surprise. They had all been trained to fight in zero-g conditions. One thing none of them had ever trained for though, was how to manage in null gravity while wearing a skirt.

"Nice legs, sugar," Toro called up to her.

Jaeger couldn't even manage to form words at the moment. All he could do was stare. Her skirt had flared out around her like the petals of a flower, leaving her legs bare and exposing the red lace panties she was wearing. He should have stayed on the catwalk to finish setting up the movie, but instead, he tossed the tablet to Toro and leaped up to join Cynder.

He didn't aim for the rope at all; he went straight for her and caught her in his arms as he floated past. She saw him coming and grabbed hold of the bag, anchoring herself so they didn't both tumble out of the bubble.

"You're a *fraxxing* lunatic," she muttered as he pulled her to him.

"If I am, it's your fault. You inspire me to acts of lunacy," he told her, then sealed her mouth with a kiss before she could say another word. Being with her inspired him to take risks again. To leap without looking; consequences be damned.

She moaned into his mouth, her lips parting as she invited him to take the kiss deeper. Her leg twined around his calf, anchoring their bodies together. He barely noticed when the lights dimmed, leaving them in near darkness.

"Did you know that was going to happen?" she asked him, laughing between kisses.

"Of course. I told you, beautiful, I had a plan. Night time for the plants means perfect vid viewing time for us."

Toro activated the tablet, and the air in front of them shimmered then coalesced into the opening scenes of the vid. The soundtrack roared to life, filling the sphere with music. Once everything was in place, Toro joined them, wrapping an arm around Cyn so she was firmly caught between the two of them.

"Popcorn?" she asked.

"In the bag. I packed it into re-sealable containers so it doesn't float away on us."

"Good thinking. They'd never let us come back if we left a bunch of popcorn floating in the middle of all this." She pulled out the popcorn, stealing a handful before handing it to Toro.

"You need anything else?" Toro asked.

"Shhh, the movie's starting," she replied before carefully tossing a piece of popcorn into her mouth.

Jaeger knew he wasn't going to be paying the slightest bit of attention to the damned movie. Not when he had Cynder so close. The three of them were floating together in the darkness; their limbs entangled as the vid played in front of them.

The night wasn't over yet, but he already knew it would be a memory he would cherish forever. No matter if they had a future together with Cynder or not, tonight was special, and so was the woman they shared it with.

CHAPTER NINE

Cynder hadn't laughed this much or felt so at ease in ages. As she floated between her dates, it occurred to her that this was the first real break she had taken in months, if not years. Before the war ended, her life had been nothing but obedience, bloodshed, and battle. Since leaving, she and her brothers had faced one challenge after another. There hadn't been time to relax or indulge in an evening of laughter and fun.

The vid was better than she expected, given it had been made in a different century. She let herself be drawn into the story, despite the two temptations floating on either side of her. For now, she was content to enjoy the moment, and apparently so were they. Their patience meant more to her than she could ever express. They were giving her the one thing she needed: control. Whatever happened between them, it would only happen if, and when, she said it could.

When the moment did come, she already knew what her answer would be. She was done denying her desires and hiding behind the wall she had built around her heart. Tonight, Jaeger wasn't the only one inspired to take chances.

It was almost the mid-point of the movie before anything happened, and when it did, it was Toro who made the first move. He removed his arm from around her waist and stroked his fingers up the curve of her spine. It was a whisper-soft caress that sent a flurry of goose flesh chasing across her back. When he reached the nape of her neck, he didn't stop; he simply reversed direction and retraced the same path. By the third pass, she had lost all interest in the vid.

She tingled everywhere Toro touched her and even places he hadn't. Anticipation built slowly, fanning the flames of her desires until she was quivering beneath his hands, and her clit was throbbing with the pounding of her heart.

Toro drew her closer and nuzzled her ear, his breath fanning over her skin. "I'm going to ask for your permission now, Cyn."

Befuddled by her overloaded senses, it took her a moment to be able to focus enough to answer him. "You already have my permission to kiss me."

"That's not what I'm asking permission for. Not this time."

On her other side, Jaeger shifted, turning toward her. He didn't say a word, but there was such fire burning in his eyes that he didn't need to speak. She knew what they were asking. What they wanted from her.

"Say it, Toro. Tell me what you want from me."

"I want you, Cyn. All of you. I want to see every naked inch of you and find out how many times we can make you come before this night has to end."

Her heart stuttered then started beating at twice the speed it had before. "Yes," she murmured. "You have my permission."

"Thank you," Jaeger said. He closed the distance between them to kiss her as Toro began nibbling on her earlobe, murmuring her name in worshipful tones. Somewhere in the distance, the movie reached a dramatic turning point as one of the lead characters declared, "I love it when a plan comes together."

All three of them laughed, and at that moment, she knew she had made the right choice. This was where she was supposed to be.

Jaeger's laughter was still buzzing against her lips as he kissed her again, his tongue teasing at the seam of her mouth until she let him inside. She speared her fingers into his hair, holding him to her as she let their tongues dance. Toro let himself drift until he was behind her as he continued to nibble and suck on her ear and the tender skin of her throat. He snaked an arm around her waist and pulled himself in tight, letting her feel the hard ridge of his cock as it pressed against her back.

She moaned, and both men reacted to the sound. They trapped her between them, stroking and kissing every inch of her body they could reach. A calloused hand stroked up her bare thigh, the roughened edges heightening every moment of anticipation as the fingers worked their way ever higher. It had to be Toro's hand on her thigh; his fingers were roughened by hours of training and lifting weights. Her theory was confirmed when Toro brushed his mouth to her ear.

"I love the lace, but it's time for it to go," he whispered.

His fingers caught hold of her panties and tore them away, the lace shredding like paper. He let them drift away, a scrap of scarlet vanishing into the darkness.

"Remind me to find those before we leave, or we'll have a lot of explaining to do, later," she said as she watched them disappear.

"I'll take care of it," Toro promised. His thick fingers moved along the curve of her hip to her waist, then across her stomach before moving down. Her breath caught in her throat as he zeroed in on his target, his fingertips grazing over her mound until he found the slick lips of her pussy.

"You're already wet for us," he murmured, his voice lowering to a husky rumble.

Jaeger reached between their bodies, stroking her breast briefly before sliding a hand beneath her skirt to test her wetness for himself. He slid a finger into her folds and groaned. "I bet you taste delicious, but I need to know for sure."

He kissed her again, nipping at her lower lip as he moved away. The lack of gravity made it necessary for them to move slowly and carefully to avoid sending all three of them tumbling out of control. Not that control was something she had much of at the moment, and judging by the harsh breathing and heated looks she was getting from her lovers, they weren't exactly cool and calm, either. The three of them were more like shooting stars, streaking across the sky in a fiery blaze of need.

Toro eased his hand out from between her thighs, stroking her clit lightly as he withdrew. The contact made her gasp, and before she could catch another breath, his hands were on her breasts, fingers teasing her nipples through the thin fabric of her top.

"No bra. Good. That's one less barrier between me and having you naked," Toro muttered. He had her shirt tugged over her head within seconds, only keeping his hands off of her for as long as it took to tuck her shirt into the bag that drifted nearby. Jaeger's hands were busy, too. He undid the clasp of her skirt, sliding it over her hips and down her legs with urgent, uneven tugs that spoke to his level of need, which started the three of them spinning.

He cursed under his breath and grabbed hold of the bag, slowing their tumble as he tucked her skirt inside. He stripped his shirt off next, and Cynder's gaze automatically fell on the spot where he had been stabbed only a few days before. There wasn't anything left but a faint scar. He didn't put the shirt away. Instead, he wrapped the cloth around Cyn's ankle before attaching it to the rope. "Now one of us is tethered."

She tugged at the knot a few times. "That'll work. Next time, though, I vote I get to tie one of you up...or maybe both of you."

His eyes lit up like a solar flare. "Any time you want me tied up and at your mercy, Cyn, all you have to do is ask."

"Same here, sugar," Toro added.

"We'll put that on the list, then," she said, slightly amazed that she was already thinking ahead to the next time.

"A list. Yeah, we're going to need a list," Toro agreed, his voice full of approval at the idea.

Before she could respond to Toro, Jaeger tugged her legs apart and buried his face into her pussy, and all the air left her lungs. There were no gentle, teasing touches or tentative caresses. He devoured her, his tongue working at her clit with long, eager strokes as his fingers parted her folds, giving him better access. She closed her legs around his head and crossed her ankles, locking the two of them together.

Toro shifted positions again, drawing her around so he could kiss her before releasing her slowly to shed his clothes. She watched as he stripped, revealing a body of sculpted muscle and power. Every lash of Jaeger's tongue took her closer to her breaking point, and by the time Toro was naked, she was bucking against Jaeger's mouth.

Toro squared away his clothes and caught hold of her hand, drawing her in close. His cock brushed her hip, and she wrapped her free hand around it, barely able to span its girth with her fingers. Toro groaned at her touch, his own hands busy toying with her breasts. The three of them began a slow dance, finding their rhythm and falling into synch with each other's pleasure.

When her orgasm came, it unfurled gradually, lifting her into a high orbit before finally launching her into a realm of pure pleasure. She loosened her legs and Jaeger withdrew, only to ease his way up her body to lay waste to her mouth with another spectacular kiss.

"We need you," Jaeger whispered against her lips.

"You can have me," she replied, meaning it with every ounce of her being. There were no more walls between the three of them. No more barriers to what they wanted.

The next thing she knew, she was being positioned between them so that she was straddling Toro's waist with Jaeger drifting beside her. Toro's hands were at her waist, and she twined her legs around him to lock the two of them together. She could feel the hard length of his cock pressed against her folds, and every part of her ached with the need to have him inside her. Their gazes locked, and she found herself lost in the dark heat of Toro's eyes as he reached between them and positioned himself to claim her.

"This is only the beginning," he told her as he rocked his hips, sending the thick head of his cock into her body.

He was big enough that he could have hurt her, but he didn't. He moved with painstaking care, letting her body adjust to him as he eased himself in deeper. He moved so slowly that by the time he was buried inside her she was ready for more. *Veth*, not only ready but eager. She needed him to move, and when he didn't, she rocked her body against his and flexed her inner walls around him.

His eyes rolled back, and he groaned aloud. "No more slow, got it."

He ground out the words as his fingers tightened their grip on her hips. Despite his words, his next thrust was almost as slow as the first one, but it was still enough to make her moan as his cock slid over nerve endings that hadn't been awakened in years. Soon they had established a give and take that kept them more or less stable while still giving both of them what they needed. Not wanting to leave Jaeger out, she caught his hand in hers and drew him closer. He still hadn't removed his pants, and she laughed as she undid them for him.

"If I'm naked, you're naked," she told him.

"Yes ma'am," he replied with a laughing salute.

One day she would ask them both about their time as soldiers. The idea of outranking them both somehow appealed to her. That was a conversation for another time and place, though.

He stripped off his pants, but before he could put them with the rest of their clothes Cynder pulled him in close and nuzzled her lips to the tip of his cock. The moment she made contact, he appeared to forget what he was about to do and let his clothing float off to join her panties somewhere in the dark.

His cock twitched and thickened in her mouth as she took him deeper, Jaeger's guttural groans telling her he was enjoying every second. She wrapped an arm around his upper thigh, and he gripped her shoulder, the three of them forming an erotic motif that wouldn't have been possible anywhere else. Time slowed, and the world beyond their perfect bubble faded into the background of her mind. Every breath brought new sensations and pleasures. Every touch triggered another round of gasps and moans as they lost themselves in each other.

Toro's body stiffened beneath her as his release started to overtake him, and he groaned her name as his steady thrusts became erratic and wild. His cock thickened in the seconds before he came, and the added friction sent her tumbling into another orgasm. Her senses were still reeling when Jaeger's hand touched her cheek, a warning that he too, was nearing his end. She rode out the last waves of her release as she hollowed her cheeks, determined to break Jaeger's control before her pleasure ended.

He shouted, his voice echoing off the walls as she took him to the back of her throat. He arched his back and came hard, pouring his salty essence into her mouth as he joined them in bliss.

None of them spoke or moved at first. As if no one wanted to be the one to shatter the moment they had just shared. They were tumbling slowly, their final, frantic movements would have sent them spiraling out of control if not for the fact she was still tethered to the catwalk below.

"Do you think they'd notice if we kept you here for a few days?" Jaeger asked.

"Maybe a week?" Toro added.

Cynder released Jaeger from her mouth but didn't unhook her arm from his thigh. She wasn't ready to let go of him completely. Not yet. "I think a lot of people would notice. For starters, you've got a fight coming up in a few days, T. Not to mention that at some point, someone will wander in here to take care of the plants. If we give some poor corporate lackey a heart attack, I'm going to feel bad. Plus, Astek will probably fine us or something for interfering with their workforce."

Toro snickered. "Good point. Can you imagine the paperwork on that? Besides, as glorious as you look right now, Cyn, I'm not keen on anyone else seeing you this way."

Jaeger's eyes darkened at the thought. "You're right, T. No one else gets to see our woman like this."

Cynder cocked a brow and stared at Jaeger. "Our woman?"

"Aren't you?" he retorted.

Toro stroked her hip. "I think you are. I mean, you're a woman, and you're with us, aren't you? I sure as hell hope you're with us. I meant what I said. I want this to be the beginning for us."

She nodded. "I'm with you. It might be a little early to be thumping your chests and utterly words like ours, though." She blew out a breath and decided to be honest. "I haven't been with anyone since I was freed. Not until the two of you."

Toro withdrew from her body and pulled himself around to her left side and cradled her close, while Jaeger shook free of her hold and reoriented himself so he was on her other side.

"No one else?" Jaeger asked.

She shook her head, feeling vulnerable after her confession.

"Then we're the two luckiest men in the galaxy. Maybe even the whole *fraxxing* universe." Toro placed a tender kiss on her forehead. "I'm glad it was us."

"So am I. If you need us to take this a day at a time, that's what we'll do. Make no mistake, though, whether I say it aloud or not, I'm still going to be thinking it. You're ours, Cynder Armas."

"Are you sure you aren't programmed for leadership, Dice? You certainly sound bossy enough."

"You know, I've always wondered about that myself," Toro said with a soft chuckle.

"So we're clear on this ours thing. It works both ways. If I'm yours, then you are both mine."

They both nodded, looking downright smug.

"If you want us all to yourself, Cyn, you've got us. No one else could compete with you, anyway. Why would we bother looking?" Jaeger asked.

"You're all I've wanted since I watched you fight the first night we met. There's not going to be anyone else."

A sense of warmth and satisfaction filled her heart, spilling over until she felt like she was damned near glowing. "In that case, I think we're officially...something. Not sure what we are just yet, but we're something more than friends."

"We're a work in progress, that's what we are," Jaeger declared.

She liked the way that sounded.

The three of them broke apart and started hunting for their drifting and discarded clothing. It took a few minutes to gather up everything before they returned to the catwalk to dress. As her lovers each slung a bag over one shoulder, she took their hands and started leading them out of the atrium.

"Where to now? I'm not ready for this night to end," Toro said.

"To my place. I believe you mentioned finding out how many times I could come before the night was over. According to my watch, morning is a long time off, which means you still have work to do." If she was going to do this, then she was going to go all the way. That meant letting them into her life, her home, and maybe, if she had the courage, her heart.

CHAPTER TEN

Toro left the ring with his arms in the air and a grin on his face. He had won another fight, which made him two for two since making his debut three weeks ago. He was on the winning streak of his life, and so far there was no end in sight. The crowd liked him, which meant heavier bets and a bigger purse at the end of the night. Even more importantly, Cynder had woven herself into his life, becoming the best part of his days and nights. She spent time with both of them, together and separately, and he treasured the moments they were together. He felt as if he had found his place at last, both as a fighter and as a man.

He had discovered he enjoyed working as club security, too. It wasn't the same intense rush as fighting, but it gave him something to do between bouts. It also paid decently, and he had added the scrip to the ever-growing amount in the bank account he shared with Jaeger. They were both putting money aside. They hadn't spoken about why. They didn't need to. They were saving up for a future they had barely dared to dream of before finding the Nova Club. They were making a life for themselves here, one they both hoped included Cynder.

One of the staff members was stationed at the door, and he opened it for Toro with a nod and a grin. "Great fight, Toro."

Toro nodded. "Thanks." He left the noise and crush of the crowd behind, but he couldn't leave his thoughts about Cynder behind so easily. So far, they were taking their relationship one day at a time, but Toro had never been one for slow and steady progress. He knew what he wanted: Cynder, in his life and his bed for the rest of his days. It was getting harder for him to stay quiet and give her the space she wanted. The three of them made so much sense, at least to him. Something was holding her back, though. In fact, the last few days he felt like she was retreating behind the walls he hadn't seen since they'd first arrived. Something had changed, and it wasn't for the better. He snarled as frustration surged through him, and he lashed out at the nearest wall, denting the metal.

"You know, most people are in a much better mood after they kick ass the way you just did. Something bothering you, T?"

His head snapped around. "Has anyone mentioned how disturbing it is to have someone pop out of the shadows the way you do?" he asked.

He hadn't gotten used to Cynder's uncanny ability to move without making a sound. She could melt into the shadows in a blink of an eye, then reappear on the other side of the room a moment later.

"It drives Kit crazy. He's threatened to tie a bell around my neck if I don't stop sneaking up on him. You, don't change the subject. You're beating up my wall, and I want to know why."

He wasn't the smartest of men, but he knew better than to tell the source of his frustration that the dent in the wall was because he wanted more from her than she was ready to give. "Just annoyed with myself is all. I was dropping my left, and it gave him a chance to score a few hits."

"We can work on it next time we're in the gym. It'll give me an excuse to go a few rounds with my favorite sparring partner."

"You never need an excuse to spar with me, you know that." He prowled over to her and set a hand on the wall on either side of her, caging her in so she couldn't disappear on him. She had done that too often in the last few days. Part of it was because work had been hectic. There had been several serious fights in the club, and at least two of them had been fueled by *crimson* overdoses. The pharma was showing up more often, and it had everyone worried and on edge.

She lifted her hands to his chest and wrapped her fingers in his shirt. "I know I don't need an excuse, but this way I have a reason that has nothing to do with how much I enjoy kicking your sexy ass. I can't stay long. It's a packed house out there. I just wanted to congratulate you on your win tonight. You were incredible."

"You have never kicked my ass, sugar. We're too well matched for that." He dipped his head and slanted his lips across hers, using the kiss to stop himself from saying anything more. He wanted to tell her she was his perfect match. He wanted to ask why she was pulling away from them. Instead, he lifted her into his arms and kissed her until he didn't have breath left to speak.

She came to him willingly, her long legs wrapping around his waist and her arms locking around his shoulders. His cock was caught between them, hard and instantly aching with need. Without saying a word, he wrapped one arm around her waist, holding her tight as he turned and headed for the door.

"I have to get back to work," she protested. Her words were a barely discernable mumble against his lips.

"They'll have to make do without you. I need you more than they do."

"Toro, I'm working!"

He ignored her attempts to wriggle out of his hold as he made for his quarters. "You got a better offer."

She laughed. "You haven't made me an offer, yet. You just walked off with me."

"You. Me. My room. Shower. Naked. Wet. Now."

"You really know how to sweet talk a woman." She leaned in and nuzzled his ear before whispering, "You've got twenty minutes. Better make them count."

He broke into a run, narrowly missing Owen, one of the security guards, as he stepped through another door.

"Sorry, Owen. We're in a hurry," she called out in apology.

The only reply she got was Owen's laughter following them down the hall.

Toro didn't stop until they were at his door, and even then he only slowed long enough to slap his palm over the access pad. He had her inside the second the door slid open, and two seconds after that she was pinned against the nearest wall so he could kiss her again. He needed to taste her, to feel her naked skin under his hands and hear her sweet cries as he brought her to orgasm. He couldn't tell her what he was feeling, but he was going to do his damnedest to show her. They belonged together. Somehow he was going to make her understand. He had to.

After two days of doubt and too much thinking, Cynder was tired. She didn't want to think anymore. It was easier to react, to give in to the yearning to be with the two men who had knocked her out orbit the day they had shown up in her club. She hadn't intended to see Toro after his fight. She had watched him defeat his opponents and instead of going back to work, she had gone to see him, knowing full well it was a bad idea. Staying away from them was hard enough already. Until she had time to digest the news Dr. Jefferies had hit her with the other day, being close to them didn't feel right, but here she was anyway. When it came to her guys, she didn't know how to stay away…even if it was the smart thing to do.

"You have clothes here, right?" Toro asked.

"Some. Why?"

He grinned and pressed his hips into hers, pinning her to the wall, and freeing up his hands at the same time. Before she could figure out what he was doing, he had her shirt in his hands. A tearing sound filled the air, and her top was reduced to two handfuls of shredded fabric.

"Really?" she asked.

"You're the one who said to hurry."

"I did, didn't I?" She wrapped her fingers in the collar of his tank top and yanked, shredding his shirt the same way he had treated hers.

"It is so *fraxxing* sexy when you do things like that." Toro cupped her breasts in his hands and leaned in to kiss her again. He was all raw need and fire tonight. His every touch a demand for her attention, his kisses hungry and hard.

"You inspired me," she told him when he freed her mouth again.

"Yeah? You inspire me, too."

He stared into her eyes, and beyond the lust burning in their depths was something deeper, something she wasn't ready to deal with. She dropped her gaze to his bare chest.

"Let's see if I can inspire you to get naked and wet. That was the plan, right?"

His brow creased, and she wondered if he was going to hold onto whatever moment they'd shared a second before. She didn't breathe again until the frown vanished, replaced by a playful grin.

"That's the plan, sugar."

If any other man ever called her that nickname, she would laugh in his face, but every time Toro said it, her heart beat a little faster. He moved back, releasing her and letting her slide back down his body until she was standing on her own. Without a word, he turned and tore off his shorts, along with the protective gear he had been wearing underneath. He dropped it on the floor and headed for the shower, giving her a stunning view of his naked body as he walked away.

"I'm going to get the water running. If I'm still alone by the time the water's hot, I'm coming to get you," he said.

"And what if I decide to skip the shower and head back to work?"

He glanced back over his shoulder and fixed her with a look so intense she forgot to breathe. "If you leave, I'll come after you. Doesn't matter if you're in the next room or halfway across the galaxy."

He was gone before she could make her brain form any kind of response. She stripped off the rest of her clothes and dropped them on the corner of his perfectly made bed, then followed after him. She was still scrambling for something to say. Some witty retort that would push him back to a safe distance without being cruel.

She was back in his arms as soon as she entered the room, which wasn't a surprise considering he took up most of the available space. There was barely room for the two of them to fit between the counter and the glass partition that formed the shower area. At least the showers were large. It was something she and her partners had insisted on when they'd had the rooms designed. Cyborgs were bigger than normal humans, and some of their staff weren't human at all. They'd made it roomy enough that even a Torski would be able to shower in comfort.

His mouth sealed over hers in a toe-curling kiss so hot it could rival a star. All her doubts and worries melted away as he held her, and she let it all go. She would face reality later. For now, all she wanted was Toro…for as long as she could have him.

They made it to the shower without breaking their hold on each other. She grabbed blindly for the liquid soap, managing to grab it on her second attempt. A quick squeeze filled her cupped hand, the slightly spicy scent filling the steamy air around them. She let her hands glide over him, exploring every inch of his powerful body and following the lines of muscle and sinew that flowed beneath his dark skin. As her hand drifted lower, he groaned her name, pumping his hips against her in silent invitation.

His cock was already primed and ready, but she moved past the thick shaft to stroke his balls, rolling them carefully across her fingers.

"Keep that up and I'm going to be inside you in a hot second," he warned her.

"Is that a threat or a promise?" She continued her caress, sliding one finger back to stroke the sensitive skin between his sac.

"Both. Either. Whatever you want it to be. Just don't stop what you're doing." He cupped the back of her head in one hand and kissed her with a passion bordering on bruising.

Toro stroked a water-slicked hand down her stomach to her pussy, using the pressure of his fingers to coax her thighs to part wider. She leaned back against the wall, using it to help her balance. The cool white tile pressed against her fevered skin, the contrast making her overloaded senses sizzle. He worked a finger into her folds and went straight for her clit, teasing the swollen bundle of nerves. Pleasure zinged through her, making it hard to think of anything but his touch. She responded in kind, stroking and touching until they were both panting and half out of their minds with need.

He shifted his hand, plunging a finger into her tight channel, and she moaned as his calloused digit curved up to hit her g-spot. The pad of his thumb pressed down on her clit, sending sparks of need racing through her. He added another finger, preparing her body for what she knew would be coming soon. Very soon, she hoped.

He tapped her thigh with his free hand. "Up."

She lifted her leg a little, and he slid a hand behind her knee, raising her leg even higher. He hooked her leg over his forearm, using his big body to steady her against the wall. "Tell me you're ready. I don't—I can't wait any longer. I need you."

She withdrew her hand from between their bodies to wrap her arms around his neck. "Need you, too."

They came together hard, the slap of wet flesh filling the air as he lifted her until his cock found its target. He groaned as he bottomed out inside her, the sound rich with satisfaction. "Hold on tight."

She nodded and locked her leg around his hip before deliberately flexing her inner walls around his cock. That was all it took to shatter his careful control. He drove into her again and again, every savage thrust pushing her higher up the scales of pleasure. His head bowed over hers, her name a broken chant that fell from his lips in time to his wild lovemaking. His cock hit every pleasure spot she had, the fierce tempo and roughness setting fire to her senses and sending her flying higher than she had ever been before.

Her orgasm came on suddenly, tearing through her with all the force of a plasma bomb. She threw back her head and screamed as her world shattered into crystalline shards of pure pleasure. Her body convulsed around his cock, milking him through his final thrusts. Toro erupted soon after, pounding into her with uneven strokes that left her feeling well used and breathless. He emptied himself inside her, and her moment of bliss was torn away as reality came crashing back.

No matter how many times she made love to Toro and Jaeger, the act would likely never lead to children. Dr. Jefferies had broken the news to her the day before, and it had shaken her more than she could have ever imagined. For the first time in her life, she was starting to imagine a future where she wasn't forever alone, and the universe had fired her fledgling hopes into the heart of a star and watched it burn. This new revelation was yet another reminder that she was a broken being whose past was never going to let her go. Toro and Jaeger deserved better. She needed to let them go so they could find someone else...but she wasn't sure she had the strength to do it.

So far, all three cyborg females Dr. Jefferies had tested were affected. The doctor had found something in their blood, a substance she had never seen before. It had taken her some time to break down what it was, and what it did. When she was certain, she had told Cynder what she had learned, along with the fact that so far, she hadn't found a way to reverse it.

Going to the corporations that created them wasn't an option. Even if they weren't the ones who had created the substance, they had to know about it. They had known and kept it a secret. Of course, Dr. Jefferies couldn't prove anything, and she would be risking her career and possibly more if she tried. Cynder didn't want that. The corporations had destroyed enough lives already.

"Cyn?" Toro's voice pierced her dark thoughts at last. "I was too rough, wasn't I?"

She stirred at last, raising her eyes to see Toro staring at her with guilt and worry gleaming in his eyes. It took her a few more seconds to figure out what he was talking about. He recognized her distress, but not the reason. "No, T. You weren't too rough. You were perfect. That was perfect."

He withdrew from her then set her carefully back onto her feet, ignoring the tiny streams of hot water flowing down his face. "You sure I didn't hurt you?"

Her heart ached, and guilt sizzled in her stomach like acid. Toro was one of the best men she had ever met. His body may have been made for war, but he had a gentle soul and a heart not even years of warfare had been able to harden. "No, baby, you didn't. I promise. I just needed a moment to catch my breath."

He frowned, clearly not convinced. She lifted a finger to his lips and smiled. "It's been a rough few days. You know that. Being with you helped me forget about it for a little while, and then it all came rushing back. That's all."

His expression softened, and he pressed a kiss to the tip of her finger. "I wish I could keep it all at bay for longer than a few minutes. If you ever want to talk about stuff, you know I'm here for you. Or Jaeger. He would probably be better at figuring out how to fix whatever's going on."

"You don't give yourself enough credit. You're an amazing, talented man, and you deserve the best of everything. Never forget that."

Toro's eyes widened, and his lips split into a grin that nearly reached his ears. "I don't care if it's true or not, I love that you think so."

Love. That single word resonated deep in her heart. *Fraxx*, no. She wasn't falling in love with Toro and Jaeger. She couldn't. She was too broken to fall in love with anyone. It would be the stupidest thing she had ever done. Not happening. Nope.

Her heart was slamming against her ribs as she rose on tiptoes to kiss him softly. "I will always think so."

He uttered a sound of pure contentment and folded her deeper into his arms. "Thank you."

She laughed. "I think I should probably be the one thanking you. You're the one who made all my worries disappear for a little while."

"I'm happy to banish your worries that way anytime you need me to. All you have to do is ask. Hell, you don't need to say a word, just crook your finger, and I'm there for you."

"I'll have to put that to the test later tonight. For now, though, reality demands my presence."

"I'd rather you stayed here with me and let me try to banish your worries again," he said even as he loosened his hold and finally let her go.

"Honestly, I'd rather stay here, too, but I can't." The truth of her words surprised her. She loved the club, especially on nights like this, but tonight there was something missing. The noise, the crowd, the buzz, none of it had energized her like it usually did.

"I know. Doesn't mean I have to like it." Toro brushed his lips to her brow, before stepping aside to let her leave.

"Come back out when you're ready. You want me to order your usual victory dinner?"

He nodded. "Steak and a beer, please. I'll see you on the floor soon."

She blew him a kiss as she left, grabbing a towel on her way to the door. She toweled, dressed, and was out the door before Toro left the shower. She had a feeling that if she didn't go before he reappeared, she might find a reason to stay with him, and that wasn't a good idea. Not until she got things figured out. If she was walking away, she needed to do it soon. And if she wasn't...If she wasn't walking away from Toro and Jaeger, she had to figure out how to tell them what the doctor had found, then hope they didn't turn and walk away from her, instead.

"Life was easier when I didn't care what anyone thought," she muttered to herself as she threw open the door to the club and let crush of the crowd distract her from everything else. She had a job to do and a business to run. Everything else would have to wait.

CHAPTER ELEVEN

Jaeger rolled onto his side and smiled down at Cynder. She was tucked in between him and Toro, still mussed and flushed from their last round of lovemaking. As far as he was concerned, this was the best part of his day: The three of them together, relaxed and entwined after a round or two of mind-blowing sex. This was when everyone's guard was down, and they talked about anything and everything as they lay in Cynder's bed and waited for sleep to claim them.

They'd shared a drink after the bar closed, toasting Toro's victory as well as a very profitable night for the club in general. While his luck at the tables hadn't been great, he managed to break even by the end of the evening. He also overheard one of the club's licensed pharma dealers offering *crimson* to some of the patrons. He let Kit know first, then notified Corp-Sec officers Mack and Dash, along with the suggestion they hurry if they wanted to arrive before Kit killed the stupid bastard for dealing undocumented product in his club.

With any luck, the dealer would be able to lead them to someone higher up the food chain, and Corp-Sec could finally make some progress on the case. Maybe then Cynder would be able to take a breath and find her smile again. He and Toro had both noticed she had been quiet the last few days, and it worried him. Everyone around her had someone they could turn to and talk with, but after spending time with Cyn, he had come to understand that she didn't lean on anyone, not even her batch brothers. If something were bothering her, she would keep it to herself and try to push through it alone. He had done the solitary route himself, more than once, and he knew it didn't work. Toro had taught him that. Now, he and T needed to show Cynder there was another way; one that had the three of them being there for each other so none of them had to be alone.

"What?" Cyn asked.

"Hmmm?"

"You're looking at me like you've never seen a naked woman before," she replied.

"I'm looking at the most beautiful woman I've ever seen, period."

"Please. I'm a sweaty, bed-headed mess at the moment."

Toro leaned in and pressed a kiss to her bare shoulder. "That doesn't mean you're any less gorgeous. Hell, since we're the ones who made you look that way, I'd say it ups the hotness factor a few degrees."

"Absolutely."

Jaeger reached out to stroke her cheek, tracing the raised edge of her scar down to her throat. "You're absolutely perfect just the way you are."

"Scars and all?" she asked, and he knew instinctively she wasn't talking about just the scar on her face.

"You wouldn't be who you are without them. None of us would be. So yes, I think you're perfect, scars and all."

She reached out to stroke her fingertips over a collection of thin scars that marked his flank. "You already know where I got my scars. Tell me about yours."

Toro snickered. "Yeah, tell her how you got that one, Jaeg. I know I never get tired of hearing the story."

"You're an asshole, you know that, right?"

"Maybe, but at least none of my injuries were self-inflicted."

Cynder raised a brow. "Oh, now I have to hear this story." She made a show of snuggling against her pillow, grinning the whole time. "Tell me a story, Jaeger."

"All right, all right." He snuck in a kiss before continuing. "We were defending some miserable hunk of rock our corporate masters had deemed strategically important. One of the other corporations was trying to take it, and we were under orders to hold it at all costs."

"That sounds familiar." Cynder sighed. "Why is it orders always came with *fraxxing* descriptions like 'at all costs,' or 'to the last man' like we were living in a vid and not fighting a real war?"

Toro shrugged. "I don't think it was real. Not to them. I heard a phrase in an old vid once that stuck with me ever since: armchair generals. That's what they were. They sat in their safe, luxurious offices on the other side of the galaxy and issued orders without ever once thinking about who they were sending into battle to die for them."

"They thought we were mindless things, interchangeable cogs in their war machine. On my sister's Termination Report, it doesn't even say she died. It states she 'ceased to function.' I hate them for what they did to us."

He was startled by the amount of venom in Cynder's voice. The few times they had talked about their past, she hadn't shown this kind of anger. Before he could press her further, she tapped her finger to his side.

"I'm derailing your story, sorry. You were telling me how you got this."

"We were with several other units, making a push on an enemy position. They were dug in at the top of a hill. Well, it was more like a heap of volcanic rock and ash than a hill. We were staying low, trying to avoid detection, and I had my head on a swivel, trying to spot potential threats."

Toro scoffed. "You still going with that lame excuse?"

He flipped his middle finger up at Toro. "Shut it. This is my story, I'm telling it my way. Now, where was I? Oh, right. I was looking out for trouble, and I slipped. Volcanic rock is nasty stuff. Some of it's as sharp as a razor. I fell on a patch of it, and it turned my side into hamburger. The medi-bots did their best, but there was a bunch of crap in the wounds...so it scarred."

"You fell off the side of a hill?" She was trying not to laugh, but he could tell it was a losing battle.

"He did. Slid ten feet down the slope, cursing the whole damned way. I had to pick him up and carry him for a half mile until the medi-bots had him patched up."

"Of course, I was cursing; it *fraxxing* hurt! There are probably still bits of me smeared across the rocks of that miserable little world."

"Where did it happen?" Cynder asked absently, still stroking his side.

"A planetoid in the Dartha system. I don't think it even had a name."

"DS-4," Toro said.

"How the fraxx do you remember the name of that—"

"What corporation did you fight for?" Cynder demanded, cutting him off.

Veth. That was a loaded question.

"Does it matter?" Toro asked.

"That's where my sister died, so yeah, it matters. We were there to take the planet from Gigan-Corp. That was you, wasn't it? You're the bastards who killed my sister!"

"We were Gigan, yeah, but that doesn't mean…dammit, Cynder, it was war! We didn't want to be there any more than you did. You know that."

She threw off the sheets and launched herself out of bed. When she turned to face them, her face was ashen, and her expression made his heart ache. Pain, anger, and betrayal, were all written across her features.

"Get out of here. Both of you."

"Cynder, please—"

"Out. Now. I can't do this. Just, get out." She pointed to the door, her hand shaking and her voice cracking as she added a final plea. "Please."

He rose from the bed and started dressing, but he didn't rush. He had things to say before she threw them out, and he had a gut feeling that if he didn't say them now, she would never give him another chance. "You said your sister was killed by a plasma grenade. It couldn't have been us, Cyn. There was a snafu with our gear, and we weren't issued any. We had nothing to do with Dana's death."

"You were there, fighting against us. Enemies. We were enemies, Jaeger! You were trying to kill my friends and me. My family. Maybe *I* killed someone you cared about, did you think about that?"

Toro got to his feet, his hands held out to her in supplication. "Cynder, please. Don't make us leave you."

"Out. Just get out," she repeated the same words over and over.

It was clear to Jaeger they weren't getting through to her. She had already shut them out. He could feel her pulling away from them more every second, and he could almost see her rebuilding the walls around her heart, making them thicker and higher than ever before. "This isn't over, Cyn. I'm not letting us end like this."

"There is no us, Jaeger. There never was. The corporations saw to that. They said they freed us, but they didn't. Not really. We're still their puppets, dangling from their strings."

"That's only true if you let it be. It doesn't have to be like that," he said.

"You don't know what you're talking about. Go. Both of you. Now, or I'm calling security."

"Cyn. Please," Toro begged. It was the first time in his life Jaeger had heard his brother plead with anyone, for anything.

"Go!"

Jaeger didn't bother with his shoes. He grabbed them and headed for the door, catching hold of Toro's arm on the way by. He sent him a message via their internal channel, hoping to convince his brother to go without argument. *"She's not going to listen to us right now. We need to regroup and come back tomorrow. We won't let it end this way. T. We'll figure something out."*

"We'd better. I'm not letting her go, Jaeg. I can't."

The short walk to the door of her quarters felt like the longest mile he had ever walked. As they reached the door, he looked back, hoping beyond hope she would give him some sign, some reason to stay.

Nothing. She was so cold, and still, she might have been carved in ice. The only sign of life he could see was the pain in her haunting green eyes. Pain that mirrored his own. They were losing her, and he didn't have the first idea how to stop it from happening.

They left in silence. Once they were in the corridor, Toro swore and slammed his fist into the nearest wall, leaving a dent the size of a small crater.

"We need to fix this, Jaeg."

"I know. Come on. We need to prove to her that we had nothing to do with her sister's death."

"How do we do that?"

"We're going to need our service records and anything we can find on the battles on DS-4. It's going to be a long night."

"I don't care how long a night it is, so long as tomorrow we've found a way to make things right again."

"We'll find a way." At least, he hoped they would, because somewhere in the middle of all this, he had fallen for Cynder. He didn't want to lose her. Not now, and maybe not ever.

* * * *

Cynder tumbled into the dark abyss of her memories, lost in grief and remembered pain. She was losing Dana all over again, lying in the battle-shattered landscape with her sister's broken body cradled in her arms. She had begged Dana not to leave her alone, giving her so many blood and medi-bot transfusions she had risked her own life to try and save Dana's. Her healing ability had been badly compromised, resulting in the scar on her face. It was a permanent reminder of that terrible day.

Losing Dana had torn open her soul. They were cloned twins, two halves of a single whole. Cyn never expected to feel whole again. Then, Toro and Jaeger came along and gave her a glimpse of happiness. It wasn't fair. One glimpse was all she got, and now she was losing everything all over again. Something snapped inside her, and she screamed aloud, giving voice to years of pain and anger. The faceless soldiers who had killed her sister weren't faceless anymore. She had met them. Laughed with them. Shared her life and her bed with them. She had betrayed Dana's memory.

Still half out of her mind, she tore through her quarters, looking for everything belonging to Jaeger and Toro. She wanted it gone, all of it. A couple of Toro's shirts. A pair of Jaeger's ridiculously expensive dress shoes. The pile started to grow. Articles of clothing, pieces of tech. The handful of dice Jaeger had been using to teach her how to play starburst. The vanilla flavored sweetener Toro liked to put in his morning coffee. There was more of it than she expected. How had they infiltrated her life so completely in only a few weeks?

She started stuffing everything into a bag, belatedly recognizing it as the one they had used to carry the picnic supplies to the atrium on their first date. Fresh pain bloomed in her chest, and by the time she was done, her eyes were watering with tears she refused to allow to fall. She dropped the bag by the door. Tomorrow morning, she would have someone deliver it to Jaeger's room. Hopefully, he would understand the message. They were done.

Tired and wrung out, she wandered back to her bedroom only to get another emotional kick to the gut. Her bed was still rumpled, and even from across the room she could detect a trace of Jaeger's spicy cologne still clinging to the fabric. Everywhere she went there were reminders of the three of them. She had to get away from it.

She looked at her watch and hoped Phyl would forgive her for the late-night call she was about to make. There weren't many people who would be willing to take on a last minute charter, no questions asked, but Phylomenia Harrington wasn't just a good pilot, she was a friend.

She would arrange things with Phyl and then let her brothers know she was taking a few days off. They weren't going to like the idea of her leaving so suddenly. They were going to like it even less when she told them she wasn't telling them where she was going, or why she was leaving, but they would just have to deal with it.

She had to get away from here. Away from them.

CHAPTER TWELVE

The door chime woke Jaeger from an uneasy doze. He and Toro had spent most of the night talking, researching, and planning their next move. So far, all they had was a stack of documents proving their unit had been on the far side of the planet from Cyn and her sister, and a shaky plan that mainly consisted of talking fast and hoping Cynder was willing to hear them out.

Not exactly a great plan, but it was all they had.

Toro rose from the couch and staggered over to the door. "I got it."

Jaeger nodded and made his way over to the small food dispenser unit. It was time for more coffee. The mug was only half full when Toro called his name.

"Jaeg. This just arrived. I think we're *fraxxed.*"

He turned, and his heart sank when he saw the bag Toro held. "Is that our stuff?"

"It looks like it." He had never heard Toro sound so defeated. "My clothes, your dice, yeah, she's sent it all back."

"No."

"No?" Toro repeated, puzzled. "No, what?"

"No. This isn't how this ends. No, I'm not letting this happen. No, she doesn't get to decide this without talking to us first. Pick one."

"How about all of them?"

"Works for me. Come on, T. We need to talk to Cynder."

They were outside her door a few minutes later. They both looked like hell, but Jaeger hoped it would work in their favor. At this point, he'd take any advantage he could get, even if it was based on pity.

He activated the chime and waited. No one answered. He hit the button again and again, nothing. Over the next five minutes, they knocked, chimed, and even tried her comm device. The door remained closed, and their attempts to contact her comm went unanswered.

Toro was hammering on the door in frustration when Zura appeared from around the corner. She approached them quickly, her silver eyes full of concern. "She's not there."

"We guessed that much. Where is she?" Toro demanded, his voice loud enough that Zura scowled at him.

"Don't take that tone with me. You might intimidate the others, but I'm married to two cyborgs that are bossier than you'll ever be. I might be able to tell you where Cyn went, but only if you calm down, quit beating on the walls, and tell me why you're looking for her."

Toro hung his head. "Sorry, Zura."

She wrapped a strand of her indigo and blue hair around her finger and nodded. "It's okay. I know you didn't mean it. Now, what the *veth* is going on?"

"We need to find Cynder," Toro said.

"Details, Toro. I am going to need more details."

Jaeger sighed. "We might have screwed things up with her a little. We want to talk to her so we can try and fix it."

"That's not likely to happen." Luke rounded the same corner Zura had come round, and Jaeger got the feeling he had been suckered.

"You set us up?"

Zura nodded. "I figured you were more likely to talk to me than them. Given that they want to punch you and all."

Kit joined them a second later. "I wasn't going to hit them…much."

"Liar," Luke said then crossed his arms over his chest and glowered at the two of them. "Care to explain why Cynder suddenly felt the urge to take an unscheduled vacation?"

"She's gone?" Toro asked.

"Two hours ago. And no, she didn't tell us where she was headed. Probably so we wouldn't be able to tell the two of you. Explain. Now." Kit took the same stance as his twin brother, arms folded and a scowl on his face.

"Not out here. Cyn wouldn't like us discussing her personal life in public." Jaeger pointed back the way the others had come. "Your quarters?"

Zura chimed in. "He's right. This is not the place to be having this conversation. Unless you're going to fight. Fight in the corridor, talk in our rooms. Anyone throws a punch once we're back inside, and I'll be pissed. I don't want to have to replace any more furniture this month."

Luke snickered. "As I recall, we weren't fighting when we broke the couch…"

"Doesn't matter. You broke it." Zura started walking. "Come on, I want to find out what happened, and you're making me wait."

Toro glanced at Jaeger and grinned. "And I thought she was a quiet, sweet little thing."

"Yeah, everyone does…at first." Kit said, his frown lessening for a moment as he watched his wife walk away. Then he glanced back at Jaeger. "If you hurt Cynder, my brother and I are going to hurt you. If you really hurt her, I'll let Zura loose on the two of you."

"I can tell you what happened with Cynder in one sentence. Toro and I fought for Gigan-Corp."

Kit winced. "Oh, *fraxx*."

"Yeah." Jaeger rubbed the back of his neck, trying to ease the tension that had settled there since his life had started imploding. "You going to be okay with that? Or should I assume I'm about to get my ass kicked for being the enemy?"

"It's not like any of us had a choice. We weren't drafted, we were designed, and we fought for whoever paid to have us created. As far as I'm concerned, our lives didn't start until the day we were freed. It's what you've done since that I care about."

"Glad to hear it." Jaeger was grateful at least one of the Armas siblings was okay with the news they'd fought on opposite sides.

Kit gave him a baleful stare. "You hurt my sister badly enough she's left the *fraxxing* station, Jaeger. What you've done since being freed might still have earned you an ass kicking."

"Please, if you were going to kick their asses you'd have already done it. Come on in, guys." Zura opened the door to her quarters and gestured for them to follow her inside.

The interior wasn't what he had expected. Zura had struck him as the type to have added homey touches to her living space. Most people, regardless of species did. In fact, the only ones he knew who didn't have much in the way of personal belongings and decorations were cyborgs and soldiers from the IAF, the Interstellar Armed Forces. It made sense. Military life had a way of making everyone a minimalist.

The walls had been painted a simple off-white color, and the furnishings were identical to the ones in the club. There were a few photos scattered around, but that was it.

She caught them looking around and laughed. "I know. Everyone who comes in here says the same thing. It's practical to use the same furniture as the Nova, and I'm not much a homemaker. Before this, the only home I'd ever known was the *Sun Sprite*."

"Ever?" Toro asked.

"You think cyborgs are the only ones who have strange lives? Try growing up with a smuggler for a father and the whole galaxy as your playground." Zura took a seat in the middle of the couch, and her husbands settled in on either side of her. "Enough about me, though. I want to know what happened. Cyn hasn't been off this station in more than a year, so if she's gone, something went seriously sideways."

"You could say that," Toro muttered as he took a seat. "How much do you know about the Resource Wars?"

"Twenty or so corporations started fighting it out for control of the resources in this part of the galaxy. When they couldn't recruit enough soldiers, they decided to make them instead." Zura gestured to the four cyborgs around her. "You guys are the result. By the time the war ended, there were only a few corporations left. Some of the remaining ones amalgamated, and now those few have enough power to be considered a ruling force on par with the galactic and planetary governments."

"Gold star, gorgeous." Luke leaned over and kissed her cheek.

"I still don't understand what the war has to do with why Cyn is gone, though," she said.

"Toro and I were created by a different corporation than your husbands. There was a time we were enemies. We were even on the same planet once."

"Oh no. Tell me you weren't on Dartha?" Luke asked.

Zura frowned. "Isn't that the system where Dana...*Veth*. What are the chances?"

"I'm a professional gambler, and I can't begin to calculate the odds, but I can tell you I would have never taken that bet. And I would have lost." He sighed. "We lost anyway. When Cynder found out, she lost it. I understand why, but I thought we'd have a chance to talk to her today. We found a way to prove we weren't anywhere near the location where Dana died." He needed them to know they hadn't been responsible. Hell, they hadn't been on the same continent at the time.

"Only she left before you could tell her." Zura sighed.

"Where did she go?" Toro asked.

Kit drummed his fingers against his thigh. "She wouldn't tell us. At the time, I wondered why, but now I get it. She knew you two would go looking for her. We can't tell you what we don't know."

They looked at each other in silence for a long stretch as they all tried to think of a way to fix this. Finally, Zura broke the peace. "I don't know where she went, but if she left the station, then she had to book transport, right?"

"You think she'd go with the easiest option?" Luke asked. Jaeger felt like he was missing something.

"What's the easiest option?"

"Phyl. Captain Phylomenia Harrington is a cargo jockey like I was, and an old friend. If Cyn was going to call anyone to get her out of here in a hurry, I bet she went to Phyl. Hang on, I'll contact her."

Zura rose from the couch and left the room to make her call, leaving the four men alone.

"Gigan-Corp, huh?" Luke asked.

"Afraid so. And you were with Vega-Axion. It feels like another life, you know?" Jaeger said.

"It *was* another life. None of us had any choice. Cyn knows that. She'll come around."

"She has to," Toro said. "She's the only woman I've ever imagined a future with. If she won't forgive us…"

"Roses," Luke said.

"Huh?" Toro replied.

"You're going to need a lot of flowers. Chocolates couldn't hurt either." Luke continued.

"A bottle of wine, maybe?" Kit added.

Luke shook his head. "Not wine. Whiskey. The good stuff. I'll grab a bottle out of the private reserve before you go after her. Don't let her throw it at you, it's *fraxxing* expensive."

"You're going to help us?" Jaeger asked. They could use all the help they could get, but he wasn't sure Cynder would appreciate her family lending them a hand. After all, right now she thought of he and Toro as the enemy.

"You clearly need it. She's been happy with the two of you, so yeah. We'll help. She helped push us into going after Zura, so we'd just be returning the favor."

"Any other advice before we go after her. I mean, assuming we can find her. The Drift is a big damned place."

"It's a big place, and she's on the other side of it. At least that's where she's headed. I was right; she called Phyl and booked transport with her. Your runaway girlfriend is on the *Beacon*."

Toro brightened. "You think she's our girlfriend?"

Zura arched a brow. "Don't you?"

"Well, we don't use that word, but uh…yeah," Toro said.

Zura stared at them. "You don't use what word? Girlfriend? Is there some sort of cyborg malfunction where none of you are capable of normal dating? It took these two months to get around to asking me out, and the first time they did, Kit wandered off in the middle of it to break up a fight. Now, you're telling me you've never even called Cynder, the woman you've been falling asleep beside every night for weeks, your girlfriend?"

"Well. No. We all agreed to take things one day at a time. It was Cyn's idea." Hearing it said aloud, he had to admit it didn't sound as logical as it had in his head. One more thing they would be apologizing for. At this rate, he was going to need to make a damned list.

Zura snorted. "Of course it was. But you went along with it. When you catch up to her, you might want to talk about that." She glanced at Luke. "Better make it two bottles of the good stuff."

"Whatever it takes," Jaeger said. He meant every word, too. He wasn't letting Cynder walk away from them. He couldn't. She was the one bright star in his dark sky, and if he lost her, he would be adrift in the dark again, and so would she.

"Good answer. She's on her way to the Torex mining platform. Phyl didn't know where she planned on going once she got there, but she's going to try and find out. I've already called Royan and told him to start pre-flight procedures on the *Sun Sprite*. He'll be ready to take off in an hour. Best you get ready." Zura eyed them both. "Maybe start with a shower."

A wave of gratitude washed over Jaeger. "You're going to have your brother ferry us across the Drift on his ship? Just like that?"

"Of course. Cynder's my sister, and you're our friends. Go get her and don't rush back. Royan can come back for you whenever you're ready. If he's on a run, I'll get one of the other pilots to pick you up. The advantage of having a shipping company is there's always a ride available when I need one."

Toro got to his feet and walked over to Zura. "Thank you," he said and wrapped her in his arms for a well-earned hug.

Three seconds later, both Kit and Luke were on their feet. "You're welcome," Luke said. "Now, let go of our woman and go find your own."

Zura laughed, hugged Toro back, and then grinned at Jaeger. "Get going before these two forget the rule about fighting in our home."

Jaeger rose and clapped Toro on the shoulder. "Let's go, T. Thank you all so much. We've been more or less on our own since the day we were freed. It's been a long time since we've had friends we could count on. Thank you. One day, I hope we can repay the favor."

"We'll talk about it once you're all back here," Kit said.

Jaeger wasn't sure what Kit meant, but right now, he had other things to worry about. Like tracking down Cynder and convincing her to give what they had a second chance. It was time to put it all on the line and go all in.

* * * *

Cynder had wandered the length and breadth of the *Beacon* half a dozen times and still couldn't settle in. She wanted to pretend it was because the ship's worn corridors and battered walls reminded her of the years she had spent being shipped from one battleground to another, or that it was the Beacon's lighter-than-usual gravity that had her agitated, but she knew better. Leaving the station, her club, and her family wasn't sitting right, and neither was the way she left things with Toro and Jaeger.

It was done, though, and there was no turning back. She would take a few days off to relax, get her emotional baggage squared away, and then return home. Maybe by then Toro and Jaeger would have moved on, or at least accepted that things between them were done and over with.

And while I'm at it, why not wish for a diamond mine or a pony? If she thought they would give up on her so easily, she wouldn't be heading for the far side of the Drift right now.

She made another circuit of the corridors, eventually winding up back at the door to the cockpit.

"You going to pace the whole trip, or are you ready to sit your ass down and tell me why I'm awake at this unholy hour of the morning?" Phyl called out from beyond the doorway.

"I thought you cargo jockeys didn't care if it was morning or night?" she said, stepping into the ship's control room.

"Who told you that? No, don't tell me; let me guess. It had to be Royan."

"Good guess. How'd you know?"

Phyl chuckled, flipped a switch on her console, and then turned in her chair to face Cynder. "He's too young to feel the effects of his hard-and-fast lifestyle, and he's as cocky as his *fraxxing* father."

Captain Phylomenia Harrington was one of Cynder's favorite people. She hadn't been out on the Drift long, but there was something about the older woman's frank manner and hard-ass attitude that Cyn clicked with right away.

"I thought you liked cocky men? You dated Royan and Zura's dad off and on for years, didn't you?" she asked, aware she was waltzing into a minefield. Still, she would far prefer to talk about Phyl's romantic past than her own.

"If the sex is good enough, a woman can overlook any number of character flaws…for a while. I was with Russ Watson for years, and believe me, it wasn't because I liked cocky, arrogant, stubborn men." Phyl pointed to an empty seat. "Since you're bolting like a scalded *peskin*, can I assume the sex wasn't good enough to keep you with your stubborn twosome?"

So much for avoidance.

"It was fun while it lasted, but I'm not looking for anything long-term."

Phyl arched one dark brow. "Uh huh. Sweetie, I've been playing poker longer than you've been breathing. Please consider that before you try feeding me another line of bullshit."

"Bull what?"

"Bullshit. Cow crap. Or as my great grandfather used to love to call it, codswallop. No, I don't know what the *fraxx* that is, but it rolls of the tongue, doesn't it?"

Phyl stretched out her long legs and fixed Cynder with a gaze that made her feel about three feet high. She briefly wondered if this was it would have been like to have a mother.

"No bullshit?" Cyn asked.

"Why bother? I'm not going to judge you, and whatever you tell me stays on this ship."

"I found out they fought for one of our enemies during the wars. The ones that killed my sister."

"You mean those two pretty boy toys of yours killed her themselves?" Phyl asked then shook her head. "They can't have, or you'd have torn their hearts out and fed 'em to them."

"No, but they were on the side as the ones who did. They were even on the planet when it happened."

"Huh," was all Phyl said.

"What?" Cynder was starting to feel grateful she had come to consciousness as an adult with most of her knowledge and behavior already encoded. If this was what having a mother felt like, she might have gotten off lucky.

"I never took you for one of those. That's all."

She blew out a breath before asking the question she already knew she wasn't going to like the answer to. "One of what?"

"A runner. When things get bad, people either run and hide, or they fight. I thought you'd be a fighter."

"I'm not running," Cyn replied through gritted teeth, not ready to admit to herself that Phyl might be right.

"And there goes my bullshit detector again."

Her hand slammed down on the arm of her chair hard enough to make the entire thing shake. "I'm not running. I'm putting some distance between us until things cool off. If I were running, I wouldn't be planning on going back."

"You don't actually think a few days apart is going to change anything, do you? I've seen the way those two look at you. If I could bottle that kind of attraction, I'd be living on a private planet somewhere instead of being an intergalactic delivery driver."

"They were the enemy," she repeated, but she wasn't even sure she believed it herself.

"From what I understand, you were all pawns in someone else's power struggle. You've said so yourself. There's another reason you're out here. Do you even know what it is?"

"It's them."

"No, it's not. *Re'veth*, you're almost as stubborn as Russ was. You sure you're not related to the

Watson family?" She snorted. "I guess we better hope not since your brothers are married to Zura. That would be…awkward."

"A little, yeah." She took a deep breath. "Do you ever regret not having kids, Phyl?"

The expressions that crossed the older woman's face were priceless. Shock, confusion, and bewilderment slammed into each other like ships on a slow-motion collision course.

When the answer came, it wasn't what she expected.

"I did have a daughter. Zura. She wasn't mine by blood, but that didn't stop me from loving her. I should never have let her drift out of my life. That's my one regret. I let my issues with her dad get in the way of having a relationship with her. If I had been around, maybe she wouldn't have gotten involved with that bastard Vin. He beat her so badly she woke up in a medical center, and I didn't even know about it. I let her down."

"But you didn't have any children of your own." It wasn't the gentlest way to say what she meant, but she wanted to understand. More than that, she needed to.

"Is that what this is about? You can't have kids?"

Her mouth opened, but no words came out. They were all locked behind the lump in her throat. She tried again. "I. No. It doesn't look like I can. The corporations did something. They broke me. More than just me, actually. Three of us so far. So you see, I'm broken, and they deserve better than that."

"You're no more broken than anyone else in this screwed up universe. Even if you were, that doesn't mean you don't deserve some happiness. If you found it, hang on tight. It doesn't come around often. Trust me on that one."

"You make it sound simple."

Phyl barked with laughter. "Simple? *Fraxx* no. Life is never simple if you're doing it right. It's messy and painful and stupidly complicated. The only things you'll have when it's over are fond memories and bitter regrets. The question you need to answer is what you want this chapter of your life to be. Memory or regret?"

"Is this what you did for Zura? Did you just parent me?" she asked before she even knew she was going to say.

Grinning now, Phyl nodded. "I do believe I did. Your first time?"

"It was. Frankly, I'm not sure I liked it. You're either really good at this or you really suck at it. Either way, I guess I have a lot to think about, huh?" Cynder's head was spinning, and she had a queasy feeling in her stomach. The same sensation she used to get after running headlong into a battle without thinking. Back then it would have been Dana giving her grief afterward for reacting instead of thinking things through.

A pang of grief hit her out of the blue. *I miss you, sis.*

Phyl got to her feet and opened her arms. "Hugs are also part of the parental nagging package."

She snickered and moved close enough to give the older woman a hard hug, and she didn't let go until the tightness in her chest eased up a little. "Thank you."

"You're welcome. Anytime you need a kick in the ass, you can always come to me. I like to feel needed. You and your brothers have made me feel welcome at the Nova. It's nice. Like I've got a home of sorts, you know?"

"Of course you're welcome. You're our friend. Hell, after this, I might promote you to our official den mother. I think we could use one."

"I'm happy to help. You can pay me back with free drinks. Deal?"

"Deal." Cynder released her hold on Phyl and took a step back. "Thanks again."

"Anytime. Am I still taking you to Torex?"

Cyn thought about it briefly, then nodded. "Yeah. I've already made a reservation for the night, might as well use it. I still need some time to work this out."

"At least, you're thinking now and not running. I'd say that's a damned good start."

Cyn reclaimed her seat. She had a lot of thinking left to do about what she wanted and how she was going to get it. For the last three years, her entire focus had been the club. Now the club was going strong, maybe it was time to find something new to focus on, like herself.

CHAPTER THIRTEEN

Toro was familiar with the Torex mining platform. He and Jaeger had spent a few weeks here when they first arrived on the Drift. It was one of the biggest stations, as well as one of the most active, out here. Most of the other stations adopted a twenty-four-hour day/night routine, but not Torex. Things never slowed down much here. There were always ships coming in with fresh loads of ore to be processed and offloaded. Shifts ran around the clock to keep up with demand and so did everything else.

The lower concourse was full of people, some of them working, most of them looking for distractions and entertainments of all varieties. Loud music blared from the bars and clubs, and brightly lit signs strobed in eye-piercing colors. The air was thick with the aroma of a dozen different restaurants and food carts; the strange combination of odors unified by the underlying scent of stale booze and hot grease. The constant assault on their cybernetically enhanced senses had been one of the biggest reasons he and Jaeger hadn't stayed on the platform for long.

"Do you remember where we're going, or do I need to call up a map?" he asked Jaeger.

"According to Phyl, she booked a room at the Corona hotel in sector seven." He looked around and then pointed to a junction coming up on their left. "That way."

He chuckled to himself as he fell in behind Jaeger. Any other woman would have chosen one of the upscale hotels in the more expensive sectors, but not Cynder. She had the means to spend a week in luxury if she wanted, but instead, she was smack in the middle of the rowdiest part of the platform. He loved that about her…even if he was still angry with her for bolting this morning.

Finding out she was gone had torn a hole in his heart.

He got that she was hurting, but *veth*, she should have given them a chance to talk to her, to explain. Walking away from them the way she had made him question if the three of them had a future after all. Why had she run? It wasn't in her nature to back down or turn tail, so why this time? He hated feeling like this. He didn't have any answers, and the only one who could give him any had gone to the far side of the Drift to get away from him.

He wanted to understand. He also wanted a drink and a couple hours in a gym to work off his frustration. *I'll settle for two out of three so long as one of them involves talking to Cyn.*

Jaeger slowed down until they were side by side again. "You okay?"

"Not really. I don't think I'm going to be until we make this right. If we can, I mean."

"Her family and friends seem to think we've got a shot at this. I'm taking that as a good sign. Besides, this is us. We don't fail, T. Not when it matters."

"I think this one matters more than all the others put together," he said, every word sinking down into his chest to add their weight to his already aching heart.

Jaeger nodded and rubbed the heel of his hand to the center of his chest. "I know."

It didn't take them long to find the place where Cynder was staying. It took a little longer to convince the fresh-faced desk clerk to give up her room number, but Jaeger eventually managed it.

"I can't believe you managed to convince that kid there's a secret cyborg branch of Corp-Sec, and we belong to it. If this ever comes back to bite you in the ass, I'm denying all part of it." Toro said as they stepped into the elevator.

"It worked, didn't it? Besides, I've heard whispers about the 'secret cyborg police' more than once. People love their conspiracy theories."

"True." He had actually managed to put aside the feeling of being an outsider. After a month at the Nova Club, he had finally gotten used to belonging somewhere again. They had friends there. It was fast becoming their home, and now even that was at risk. If Cynder wouldn't talk to them, they'd have to move on. Maybe not right away, but there was no way he could stay and watch her live her life without them.

The closer they got to her door, the tighter the knots in his chest got. He hadn't felt like this since his days in combat. The battles where everyone knew the odds were ugly, and it was a given that not all of them would be alive when it was over. Back then, he fell back on his training and abilities as a soldier. This time, he was going in unarmed and with no idea how to proceed.

"All things considered, I think I'd rather be heading into combat than her hotel room," he said.

Jaeger chuckled. "Yeah, T. Me, too. This isn't anything we ever trained for."

Toro reached the door half a stride ahead of Jaeger. He squared his shoulders and rapped directly on the door, ignoring the courtesy chime on the panel.

No one answered. *Not again. She has to be here.*

He raised his hand and started to knock again, only to have the door slide open while his hand was mid-knock.

"I knew it was you. Everyone else uses the chime; you just dent the door until someone opens it."

He lowered his hand. "Hi, Cyn."

"Hi. I'd ask how you found me, but that's pretty obvious. Phyl told Zura, and Zura told you, which means Little Blue and my brothers must be on your side." She looked tired, which wasn't surprising. Sleeplessness seemed to be making the rounds these days. She was dressed in black from head to toe, from her scuffed combat boots to the black leather bodice she wore over a pair of form-fitting jeans.

She looked incredible and the slightest bit vulnerable. It gave him hope.

"There don't have to be sides at all. I don't want there to be," he told her.

She looked at him, then Jaeger and nodded. It was almost imperceptible, but it was there.

"We don't always get what we want, T," she murmured.

"Sometimes, we do. Can we come in?" Jaeger asked. "Please?"

Again, the tiny nod. "Okay."

He was through the door the second she stepped back. He wasn't going to give her any time to change her mind. He wasn't leaving until they'd talked. All of them. About everything. When he walked through the door again, he wanted it to be with Cynder by his side.

Cynder wasn't really surprised to see them at her door. She hadn't expected them to arrive so soon, though. Phyl must have tipped them off to her location before her ship had even left Astek.

She thought she'd have more time to think about things. Apparently, her time was up.

"You shouldn't have left like that," Toro said. He didn't take a seat. Instead, he set his bag down on the floor, leaned his big body up against the doorway, and then folded his arms over his chest. She suspected nothing short of a hull breach would make him move until he was ready.

"You're right. I'm sorry I left the way I did." She sat down in a slightly battered chair, leaving the couch for Jaeger. She still needed to keep her distance. Seeing them again, both of them looking so tired, wary, and bruised, made her want to curl up in their arms and skip talking altogether. They might have been the ones who hurt her, but she hurt them, too. She could see it. She wanted to go to them. Touch them. Hold them and let them comfort her while she did the same for them. But first, they had things to talk about. More than either of them knew.

Fraxx. What a mess.

Jaeger took a seat on the couch and started rummaging through his bag. "We spent all night working on something for you. We wanted to prove to you we weren't anywhere near you or your unit."

"You did?"

"Of course we did. You accused us of being involved in your sister's death. No matter what comes of us, you have to know that isn't what happened." He handed her a data tablet. "We were on the other side of the starsforsaken planet, Cyn. It wasn't us."

She took the tablet but didn't read it. There was a lot she wasn't sure how to say, but this was one thing she had already decided. Even if they had been there. Even if they had thrown the plasma grenade themselves, it didn't matter. It was war, and none of them had any choice. "I regret saying what I did. It wasn't fair of me. None of us chose to be there. We didn't sign up to fight. We didn't get to pick a side. For all I know I could be the one who killed someone you cared for. I was a sniper. I ended a lot of lives in the ten years I fought. We all did."

"I hated it. What they made me do. What they made *us* do." Toro pointed to the tablet in her hand. "Read it, please. So you never have doubts about it. As far as we can tell, your unit and ours never crossed paths. Not once."

She scanned the information on the screen. Dates. Locations. Coordinates. There were gaps, of course. Even now that the wars were over, the corporations guarded their secrets with care. Still, it was obvious from what information they had found that they were right. They had never faced each other in battle. All three of them had blood on their hands, but this proved that none of it belonged to someone they had loved.

"You see?" Toro asked.

"Yes." She set the tablet aside, and with it went a heavy weight she hadn't even known she carried.

"You were right. I needed to see it. I don't know how you managed to pull all of that together so quickly."

Jaeger's mouth curved up into a ghost of a smile. "We were very motivated."

"And then we got interrupted by one of your employees delivering our stuff back to us," Toro said.

She didn't have to look at him to know he was scowling at her. "I'm sorry about that, too."

"We shouldn't have left you alone. You were hurt and angry, and we should have stayed with you. I'm sorry we left, Cyn, but we were coming back. Why didn't you wait and talk to us? Why are we here, on the far side of the Drift?"

"I made you leave. I screamed at you and called you killers. You two didn't do anything wrong. This is on me. I didn't—There's stuff—I didn't even get what I was really doing until I was halfway here. I thought I was doing the right thing, but then Phyl did some sort of maternal mind-trickery thing and made me see I wasn't. She said I was running away…and she was right."

Jaeger leaned forward bracing his arms on his thighs. "What are you running from, Cyn? Us? The war? I thought things were going well, and then all this happened, and you were gone. Why?"

"Because the corporations aren't done destroying my life yet. I'm more broken than even I knew, and I knew I was pretty *fraxxed* up. I thought you deserved better, and I didn't want them derail your lives, too," she said. The entire statement came out in a single, hurried breath that even she barely understood.

It took Jaeger and Toro a few seconds to catch up, but once they did, their response made her regret ever trying to push them away.

"What's destroyed? What have they done? Why didn't you tell us?" Jaeger demanded.

Toro straightened, a stormy look in his dark eyes. "No one is going to ruin your life. I won't let that happen."

The explanation came out in a hurried tangle. "Dr. Jefferies. The test she did. I got back the results a few days ago. No kids. Not for me, not for the others she's tested. There's something in our blood. Something she thinks the corporate lab rats put there. The bastards broke me even more than I knew. I thought I was free of them, but I'm not. I can't ever be, because they didn't just make me a killer, they made sure I could never be anything else. I can't create life, I can only take it."

The room fell silent in the wake of her inelegant confession.

"You left because you found out you can't have kids? That's why we had to chase you across the *fraxxing* Drift?" Toro demanded.

"I'm going to spank your ass for that at some point. You should have told us. That's not the kind of thing you brood on, alone. You got it? No more brooding. No more running. It's not good for my ego to have to chase the woman I love around cosmos."

"You love me?" she barely recognized the voice asking the question as her own, and even as she said it, part of her was wincing at the way it sounded. When had her life become a scene from a vid…and a cheesy one at that?

"You're not seriously going to ask us that, are you?" Toro asked, moving away from the door at last. "We're here, aren't we? And for the record, I don't care if you can have kids or not. You're not broken, Cynder. You're perfect. Don't ever forget that. To me, you're always going to be perfect."

They moved at the same time. Jaeger rose from the couch as Toro strode across the room to stand at his brother's side. They both dropped to their knees in front of her, identical looks of frustration, longing, and love on their faces.

"I told you if you left, I'd come after you. I will always come after you because I love you," Toro said.

Jaeger turned and grinned at Toro. "What he said. I can't improve on that, so I'm just going to agree. We love you, and we're not going back to the Nova without you."

"I thought we weren't doing this? One day at a time, remember?" she asked, trying to ignore the rapid tripping of her heart and the lump in her throat.

Toro took her hand, gripping it tight. "That was what you wanted. I was never in this for a day at a time. I'm greedy. I wanted forever from the first second I saw you fight. I just never thought there was a chance I could have that. Not with someone like you."

"Why would you think you couldn't have that?" she asked him. This wasn't only about her anymore. Something bigger was happening. Something important. She wasn't the only one hurting and full of doubts.

He thumped his free hand to his chest. "Because of what I am. I was created to fight. That's it. No other skills. You think you're broken, but I know what I am: incomplete. They only gave me what they thought a killing machine would need and left the rest out. What kind of woman would want to spend her life with someone like that?"

"You're not incomplete. You might have been in the beginning. I can't say for sure because I didn't know you back then. All I know is the man you are now, and there's nothing missing from him. He's strong, and brave, and kind, and gentle. They didn't teach you any of that. You taught yourself. You made yourself whole."

"You can see it in him, but not in yourself." Jaeger took her other hand, but his touch was gentle, almost tentative. "You need to stop judging yourself by who you were and start seeing who you are now."

Toro snorted. "Good advice. Too bad you refuse to see it applies to you, too."

She knew what Toro was talking about. Jaeger didn't simply think of himself as broken. He believed he was unworthy of the life he had. He hadn't forgiven himself the lives he took while they were soldiers. *Veth*, she had even called him a killer and accused him of murdering her sister. Icy tendrils of horror and shame coiled tightly around her heart. Her accusations had added to the guilt and pain he already carried.

Jaeger shook his head. "It's different for me. You two were doing what you had to because there wasn't any other choice. Me? I was good at it. Hell, I enjoyed it. The technical details, the precision. I was always pushing myself to improve. Do you understand? Every time I improved, it meant more people died. There's no redemption for that."

"It was part of your programming, wasn't it?" she asked softly.

Jaeger stared into her eyes, his fingers tightening on hers as if he expected her to pull away. "That's no excuse."

"It has to be. If it isn't, then I'm never going to be able to live with the things I've done. I was a sniper. I killed from a distance. An unseen threat in the shadows, watching and waiting until I knew my targets' faces better than any lover's. It was what they made me for."

The words she needed to say stuck in her throat, but she forced them out anyway. If they were going to be honest, then she couldn't hold anything back. Not even the things she barely acknowledged to herself.

"I don't know what it was like for the female cyborgs you knew, but I was programmed to consent to every request for sex that came from someone on our side. Soldiers. Lab techs. Corporate suits. Anyone. Everyone. I enjoyed it, because that was part of my programming, too. So, don't you dare tell me our behavior programming isn't an excuse. It has to be. I *need* it to be."

Jaeger's eyes widened, and both of them gripped her hands tighter. "That's not the same thing!"

She shook her head, determined to drive her point home. "You don't get to pick and choose. Either we were compelled by our programming, or we weren't. If you can forgive me, you have to forgive yourself."

"There's nothing to forgive," Toro declared before leaning in to brush a tender kiss to her mouth. "You said I've become more than they made me to be. If that's true, then the same goes for you. Both of you."

"You're not playing fair, you know," Jaeger said.

"Nothing's fair in love or war. Isn't that the expression?" she replied.

"So, which is it? Love, or war?" Toro asked.

She beamed at them. "It's love. I love you both so much. I don't know what happens next, or how we're going to make this work, but whatever we have, I'm in until the end."

Jaeger grinned. "What happens next is easy. We're taking you to bed. If this place has room service, then we're not leaving for days. If not, then we'll let you up…eventually."

"That's not what I—hey!" she yelped in protest as Toro tugged her into his arms and then rose to his feet, taking her with him. He draped her over one shoulder and clamped a hand down on her ass, holding her in place. It was only a few steps to the bed, and when they got there, he tossed her gently onto the center of the mattress.

"Stay," he said, pointing at her with a stern expression that belied the laughter in his dark eyes.

"Careful, T. I love you, but that doesn't mean I won't kick your ass if you try and tell me what to do."

"The last time I let you out of my sight, you vanished. I'm not letting that happen again." Toro started to strip his shirt off, stopping just before the fabric passed over his head. "You better still be on that bed when this comes off."

"Or what?" she challenged him. Not that she had any intention of going anywhere without them. Not now, and quite possibly not ever again. Having them back in her orbit put everything into perspective. When she had left them behind, nothing had felt right. She still missed her batch brothers and even the non-stop insanity that was the Nova, but the hole in her heart had started to heal when she had opened the door and found Jaeger and Toro standing there.

"Or we track you down again. Then maybe we tie you to the damned bed to make sure you stay put," Toro said as he tossed his shirt aside.

"That's not much of a threat. You've already tied me up once, remember?"

"I'll never forget that night."

"Me, either." Jaeger kicked off his pants and joined her on the bed, wrapping her in his arms and snuggling her against his naked body. "Everything about that evening was unforgettable."

It felt good to have him holding her again.

"It was," she said, resting her head on his bare chest.

"Maybe while we're here, we can make some new memories," Toro said as he stripped off the last of his clothes.

The sight of his hard, sculpted body and the love shining in his eyes made her wonder how she ever thought she could walk away from him. From either of them. Toro joined them on the bed, his touch tender as he cupped her cheek in his hand and kissed her. This was what she wanted the rest of her life to be like. The three of them together, supporting and loving each other. It didn't matter if she couldn't have children. Even if it was only the three of them, they could still be a family.

* * * *

Jaeger was the weariest he had ever been. It wasn't the physical drain of the almost sleepless night followed by the trip across the Drift to chase after Cynder. His medi-bots could keep him on his feet for days if necessary. It was the emotional roller coaster he was on that had him reeling. In all the years since his release, he had moved forward without ever dealing with the past. He buried his guilt and regret deep in the back of his mind and left it there, hoping it would die a quiet death. Wishful thinking. He knew that now. Hell, he had known it then, too, but he had ignored everything anyway.

Now, he was paying the price. Falling for Cynder meant dealing with the past. It might have been easier to keep everything boxed away, but that wasn't going to work. Not anymore. Not for any of them. The trouble was, he had been carrying those buried feelings around for so long, it wasn't going to be easy to let them go. Cyn was right, though, he didn't get to pick and choose what got forgiven. It was an all or nothing deal. For her, he would make it work somehow.

"I don't think we thought this through. Now you're both naked, and I'm dressed. You're going to have to let go of me so I can get naked, too, and I'm too damned comfy to want to do that," Cynder muttered without moving an inch.

"Then don't. I think between the two of us, we can figure out how to get you naked. I'm not keen on the idea of letting go of you right now," he said.

"Me either. And as it happens, this hot little leather thing you're wearing has the laces in the back."

"I'll start on her boots, and we'll meet in the middle." Jaeger pressed an open- mouthed kiss to her bare shoulder before moving down to her feet. He wanted her, but it wasn't the time for sex. They were all raw, tired, and ragged after the events of the past day. There would be time for bed sport later. For now, he wanted to take care of her, to protect and cherish her in every way he could. He had never felt this way before. Everything that happened from now on would be unfamiliar territory, for all of them. They would have to find their way together.

He took his time undressing her. Stripping away boots, jeans, and finally, the tantalizing bit of silk and lace beneath. He sent a quick message to Toro, suggesting they pamper their girl, and his brother responded with a brief nod.

When he was done, he moved back down to her feet and lifted them into his lap. When she looked up in confusion, Toro kissed her and then murmured in her ear, so softly he could barely make out the words.

"We're going to take care of you, sugar. Lie back and enjoy it."

"But—" she started to protest, so Toro kissed her again, cutting her off.

"Shhh. There's no rush, is there?" he asked, pressing his knuckles into the arch of her foot.

She let out a low moan and shook her head.

"That's right. You came out here for a break, right? Indulge yourself a little, Cyn."

She didn't speak, but some of the tension left her body, and she settled back onto the bed. The bodice she'd worn had been laced tight enough that there were red marks on her skin, and Toro started to kiss each and every one of them while Jaeger focused on massaging her feet.

Soon the rhythmic touches and caresses had him feeling almost as relaxed as she was. He worked his way up her legs, and when Toro coaxed her to turn onto her stomach so he could reach her back, she did so without a word of argument. They worked together, kneading and stroking her until she was uttering soft, sleepy sighs of contentment. For him, there wasn't a more satisfying sound in the galaxy.

They didn't stop until Cynder was close to falling asleep. Moving together, Jaeger lifted her off the bed and cradled her in his arms while Toro pulled back the covers. They got into bed and settled her between them, and that was when she finally stirred. Her eyes opened slowly, and a sense of déjà vu hit him hard as she smiled up at him. They had come full circle, back to last night. Before all it all went to hell.

"You're doing it again, Diceman. Looking at me like I'm the only naked woman you've ever seen."

"I'm never going to stop looking at you that way. You're too beautiful."

"From now on, you're the only naked woman we're going to see. Our girlfriend, the sexy, ass-kicking cyborg."

"I'm your girlfriend?" she asked, slightly dazed.

"I think we're past that bit. We love you; you love us. If that doesn't make you our girlfriend, what does?" he asked, amused by her reaction.

"Well, *fraxx*. That seems logical. I should probably warn you, I've never been anyone's girlfriend before."

"And I've never been in love with someone before. We're all in over our heads, beautiful."

"You're sure you want to do this? It could get messy," she asked.

"Never been surer of anything in my life," Toro said.

"Me either. We'll worry about everything else later. After we've gotten some sleep." He kissed her cheek and then settled in beside her. With her in his arms, maybe he would finally be able to sleep again.

CHAPTER FOURTEEN

It was Cynder's hunger that finally forced her to wakefulness. When she opened her eyes, several facts hit her at once. She wasn't in her room, she was naked, and she wasn't alone. A very big someone was in bed with her, and he was as naked as she was. She turned her head, relaxing again when she recognized Jaeger. He was still asleep, but even unconscious, he was holding her close, his arm crossing her waist and his body spooned up tight behind hers. At least one of her guys was here with her, but where the hell was here, exactly?

A quick look around filled in some blanks. Bland, white walls. Thin pillows. A bedspread with some sort of faded orange and yellow sunburst pattern on it and not a scrap of blue in sight. She was definitely not anywhere in the club. Recollections of the past twenty-four hours trickled in slowly as she came fully awake. She groaned as everything fell into place. Where she was and why she was there. The fight, the trip with Phyl, and finally the long, emotionally charged conversation with the men she loved.

Loved. *Whoa.* That thought had her heart beating fast and hard against her ribs. She loved them, and they loved her in return. Both of them.

Both…she sat up and looked around the hotel room. There was no sign of Toro. She checked her watch. They'd been asleep for three hours. Not long at all.

"Jaeg, wake up. Where's T?" she said, twisting out of his embrace so she could roll over and face him.

"Hmm?"

"Toro's gone. We should go find him."

Jaeger cracked open an eye. "Or I could ask him where he is without leaving this nice, comfy bed. You might not want to be linked to your siblings via your internal comm channel, but it does come in handy sometimes."

"My brothers are bossy pains in the ass. Would you want your former commanders in your head all the time?"

"If it meant we'd tracked them down, then yeah. I'd put up with the chatter. At least for a while. You know, we could add you to our comm channel. That way you'd be able to talk to us even if we weren't together."

She opened her mouth, intending to say no, but she stopped herself. Instead, she asked, "Can we do that? I know we were all more or less designed the same because everyone was stealing each other's ideas and reverse engineering every technological advancement, but we weren't on the same side. Wouldn't they, I don't know, want to make sure we didn't talk to each other that way?"

"I know it's possible. When our batch was decimated in a raid, they merged us with the remnants of several other batches. Some of those soldiers were from a smaller corporation we'd already defeated."

"We'd still need a lab tech to do it." The idea of letting one of them near her made Cynder's skin crawl. After everything the corporations had done to her, she couldn't imagine putting herself in the hands of one of their people.

"I'd never let a tech come near any of us again. Not if I had any choice. I think I can figure it out, given a little time. It can't be as tricky as building a bomb, right? Dr. Jefferies might know where I can get the information I'd need."

"I'll think about it. Once you know more, we'll talk about it again."

"I'll find a way. I like the idea of being able to whisper dirty, sexy things to you while you're up in your office, working on boring paperwork."

Her still slumbering libido came awake with a roar at his words. "If you did that, I'd never get any work done."

"You work too hard. A little playtime would be good for you."

"Playtime isn't what I want. I want time with you and Toro. Speaking of T, you find him yet?"

"I got distracted by the naked woman talking to me. Hang on a second."

Jaeger was silent for a few seconds. "He says he couldn't sleep and went to blow off some steam. He's working out at a club he used to fight for. Wants to know if we can meet him for dinner in an hour or so."

"He left to go work out?" A dark flower of doubt bloomed in her heart. Why had he left? Was he having second thoughts already?

"He wants me to tell you that he only left because you needed rest. He'd rather—and please remember these are his words, not mine—he would have rather been pounding you than a punching bag."

"Tell him next time, wake me up," she said, relieved and amused at the same time.

"Done. And by the way, this proves my point about you needing to be linked to us. I'm not spending the rest of my life relaying messages between the two of you."

"The rest of your life, huh? You sure? We don't even know how long our lifespans are. The doc's best guess is we'll still be in our prime at one hundred years old. That's a long time to commit to one woman."

Jaeger cupped his cheek in her hand and gave her a look that turned her insides to molten gold. "I'm sure I want to spend the rest of my life with you. I don't care how many years we have together, it isn't going to be long enough."

Love and desire flared up together and fused into something new. Something stronger than anything she had ever known. She turned her head and brushed a kiss to the heel of his palm. "For a man who has never been in love before, you certainly know the right things to say."

"I'm always this charming, haven't you noticed?"

She laughed and nipped at his hand. "I must not have been paying close enough attention." The truth was deeper than that. Jaeger was charming on the surface, but it was a glib, glossy charm with no depth. What he said to her a moment ago wasn't glib. It was something heartfelt and real. It was the real Jaeger, and she loved him.

"Minx." He kissed her hard, but before she could kiss him back, he moved away again. The next thing she knew he had thrown the covers off them both and flipped her onto her stomach.

"What are you doing?" she asked.

"Collecting on a debt I'd forgotten about until now. I did say you were going to get spanked for leaving us without a word."

"Don't you even think about—"

Smack. His hand came down on her ass with enough force to burn, but not quite enough to hurt.

"What happened to your vow of non-violence?" she demanded, not sure if she was more pissed off or turned on by what he was doing.

All she got in response was a dark, sensuous chuckle that flowed over her, sending a bolt of raw need straight to her clit. He stroked the spot where his hand had struck, and she discovered that the skin there was more sensitive to his touch.

The next blow hit her other cheek, and this time, he put a little more force behind it, enough to make it sting. To balance it out, he spent more time soothing the spot with his fingers afterward. By the time the third one landed, there was no denying that she was turned on. Her skin was tingling, and her clit was throbbing, aching to be touched. She slid her hand between herself and the mattress, intent on making herself come.

"No," Jaeger growled. "Keep your hands on the bed. When you come, it'll be my touch that does gets you off, not yours."

"You're enjoying this way too much," she grumbled. She was trying to sound indifferent, but that was hard to do when the next crack of his hand made her moan aloud.

"We're both enjoying this." He caressed her heated skin, slowly moving his hand along the seam of her ass to her soaking wet pussy.

She lifted her hips, trying to get him closer to where she needed his fingers, but he slapped her ass again. "Don't move."

She twisted her head around to glower at him. "Don't push your luck."

"Let it all go and trust me, Cyn."

Doubt blossomed again, staining her thoughts. She wasn't good at letting go. "I don't...I've never..."

"I know. I don't either. It's something we're both going to have to work on. It's not going to happen all at once, but if we're going to work, we're going to have to trust each other."

A wicked thought formed. "I'll do this, but one day you're going to let me tie you up. Deal?"

He hesitated for the barest of seconds, but it was enough for her to know that this wasn't easy for him, either. "Deal."

His fingers started moving again, one hand caressing her still sensitive skin while he worked his other hand between her legs. She parted her thighs, giving him the room he needed without moving more than she had to. He rewarded her with a firm press of his fingers against her clit. She moaned again, tangling her fists in the sheets as a wave of bliss washed over her.

When the next blow came, she had to bite back a scream. Pleasure and pain came together in an explosion that left her teetering on the brink of an orgasm. He had to know it, too, because he didn't give her a chance to recover before he slid two fingers into her channel and smacked her again.

She didn't simply come; she came apart. For one brief but perfect moment, she was nothing but a collection of sensations. Everything else vanished. The club, *crimson*, her infertility. There was no past to run from. No loss or regret. It was bliss, and she held onto it as long as she could.

"You still with me?" Jaeger asked when she finally came down from her high.

"Barely." She managed to open her eyes, but that was all. The rest of her body was still trembling with the aftershocks of her orgasm and didn't seem to want to move yet.

He stretched out beside her and then drew her in close enough he could nuzzle her ear. "I'm never going to tire of watching you do that."

She rolled onto her side and wriggled up against his chest, deliberately grinding her ass against the hard shaft of his cock.

"Teasing me again?" he asked, his voice little more than a strangled groan.

"Mhmm."

"Dangerous. How did that end for you last time?"

"With the best orgasm of my life. If you're trying to make an argument for me playing it safe, you're doing it wrong."

Hot breath fanned over her skin as he pressed several kisses to the side of her neck. "Best of your life, huh?"

"Top three, anyway." This was what she loved best. Not that the mind-shattering sex wasn't great, but it was the rapport she shared with the two of them that truly made her happy. She could see herself spending the rest of her life teasing and laughing with the two of them, and it filled her with a sense of joy she'd never imagined possible.

"Let's see if we can hit the top spot, together."

The embers of desire rekindled instantly. "Yes, please."

He ran his hand down her side, over her hip, and along her thigh with painstaking slowness. When he reached her knee, he drew her leg up then over so it was draped over his. Still moving with measured precision, he let his hand drift down, between her legs. He stroked her clit with his thumb, moving it in maddening little circles until she was slick, wet, and eager. Only then did he move into position, the wide head of his cock breaching her with the same exquisite slowness.

"I love you," he whispered as he filled her an inch at a time. "I want to make love to you every day for the rest of my life. We're programmed for loyalty, to devote ourselves to a cause. Loyalty to my corporation was never my choice; they were my default. You're my cause, Cynder. *You're* my choice."

Her body sang with pleasure, but her heart was lifted by another song. Love and joy filled her to overflowing. "You're my choice, too. Both of you."

"Mine." His arms closed around her, hands on her breasts, breath in her ear. He rolled his hips, surging deep into her body, and she rocked back at the same time, driving their bodies even closer together.

The heat built between them slowly, their tempo unchanging. Glide and thrust. In and out. Slow and sensual, his thick cock stroking along her inner walls, igniting a firestorm of passion and need that consumed everything around her. She reached back, sinking her nails into the flesh of his hip and he responded with a low groan of her name.

Teeth nipped at her throat, the scruff of his beard scratching her tender skin. He sucked on her neck, and she laughed, aware he was doing it deliberately. "Marking your territory? Aren't we supposed to be a more enlightened species than that?"

"No man of any species is enlightened when it comes to a beautiful woman. It's too soon for a ring, right? Until then, this will have to do."

She tried to think of a response, but it wasn't possible to follow any thought more than a few seconds before it vanished beneath another wave of pleasure. She gave up trying to talk or think. She let go of everything but him, and he carried her with him to the heights of ecstasy. Her release was as slow as their lovemaking, unfurling like a flower in the first light of dawn.

He came hard, locking his arms around her as he shuddered to a climax that went on for what felt like an eternity. Breathless and trembling, she closed her eyes and waited for the world to come back into focus. Neither of them spoke for a while. Both of them basking in the last precious moments of bliss.

"Top two?" he asked.

"Seriously? That's what you're thinking about right now?" she retorted, flexing her hand so that her nails bit into his hip again.

"I can think about more than one thing at once, you know. I'm also thinking about what to have for dinner once I let you out of here."

She laughed. "Very romantic."

"Well, you can take it as a given that I am always thinking about you."

"In that case, yes, definitely the top two. And I was thinking I want breakfast for dinner. Maybe waffles. With blackberry syrup."

"Who has blackberry syrup way the hell out here?"

"Hmph. Good point. I'll have eggs benedict instead. Everyone has hollandaise sauce. Of course, neither of us is going anywhere until we shower, and to do that, you have to let go of me," she pointed out.

"If it weren't for the fact I'm starving, I'd refuse to let you go. However, I haven't eaten anything since last night, and I'm betting you haven't either, so… food wins."

"For the first time in my life, I wish I had splurged for a place that had room service. Then we could stay here, eat, and tell T to get his ass back here."

"Next time, we pick a place with room service."

"Next time, we'll pick our destination together." It was strange to talk about their future so easily after the darkness and doubt of the last few days. She could never have imagined things would work out so well. If not for Phyl's advice, things might have been far different. She was going to buy Phyl dinner when she saw the pilot again, and maybe even give her another hug.

Jaeger swatted her still tender ass and jumped out of bed. "Race you to the shower. If we're quick, we might have time to take another shot at the top three before we have to meet Toro."

She bounded after him. "Last one in buys the drinks!"

CHAPTER FIFTEEN

Toro rolled his shoulders and tried to stay focused on the fight to come. He ignored the jeers and calls of the crowd surrounding him. They didn't matter. He had fought here before, a few months ago. The crowd hadn't been any friendlier back then. They were a rough lot who liked to drink hard and play harder, and some of them had a strong dislike for cyborgs. They saw Toro and his kind as outsiders, freaks who threatened the status quo. It was a foolish fear. Even if the cyborgs had wanted to take their jobs, there weren't enough of them in existence to claim even a fraction of the work available on the Drift.

Their bias and hostility had been enough to make he and Jaeger move on, a decision that eventually led them to the Nova Club and Cynder. Toro grinned. Cynder was the reason he was back in the ring tonight. He hadn't planned on fighting; he only wanted to work off some of the stress of the past day. When he had shown up at a bar called the

Pit, the owner had offered him a huge payout to fight. They were down a fighter, and the scrip had been too much for him to resist.

He had already spent the money on a gift for Cynder. He wanted to give her something special, and the offer to fight gave him the means. Torex was primarily an ore processing station, which meant there was a vast selection of gems and precious metals on hand. He had forgone his workout to prowl the jeweler's sector until he found what he wanted.

"We're here. Where are you sitting?" Jaeger's voice sounded in his head, and Toro cursed. They weren't supposed to be here until *after* the fight.

"You're early. I haven't got us a table yet. There was something I needed to do first."

"Where are you? This place is a madhouse. Why did you want to meet here anyway? Feeling nostalgic?"

"I can't talk right now. Tell Cyn…fraxx. Tell her she can kick my ass later."

"What did you do, T?" Jaeger demanded.

Toro didn't bother answering. The cheers of the crowd announced the arrival of his opponent and all his attention was on the massive Torski joining him in the sunken fighting area that gave the bar its name.

No wonder the guy he was replacing opted to be somewhere else tonight. He had fought this species before, but this one was in a league of his own. Torskis were heavy gravity worlders, and most of them were between seven and eight feet tall, tipping the scales at around eight-hundred pounds. This one was closer to eight and a half feet and had to weigh half a ton. *Veth*. This is going to hurt.

The first punch came before the bell had even sounded to officially starting the match. Toro managed to block it, but the Torski came at him like a runaway comet. All he could do was defend himself from a flurry of wild swings and ham-handed blows coming his way. His opponent had no fighting technique at all. He was pure rage and violence. Toro started hitting back, expecting the big alien to back off or at least raise his guard. The opposite happened. Every blow he landed only seemed to ratchet his opponent up another notch. This wasn't a typical fight; it was a no-holds-barred brawl. If he was going to win, he was going to have to stop playing by the rules.

He lashed out with a foot, catching the Torski square in the chest and knocking the brute back a few steps. When he came at Toro again, his movements were jerky and uneven, his gait unsteady. As the big alien bared his fangs and bellowed in frustrated fury, Toro finally clued into what he was dealing with. His opponent was out of his mind on some sort of pharma, mostly likely *crimson*. Winning this fight wasn't his biggest worry anymore; walking out of here in one piece was.

* * * *

Jaeger heard the roars of the crowd and looked over to the fighting pit with a sinking feeling in his gut. Toro wouldn't...would he? He spotted his batch brother in the sunken arena and cursed. *"Re'veth."* Apparently, he had. What the hell was he thinking?

"Tell me I'm not seeing this," Cynder said.

"I'd love to be able to do that, but I'd be lying."

"Did he forget he's under contract to the Nova?"

"Actually, he's not. The thirty-day contract expired, and you two haven't gotten around to signing the extension It's been sitting on your desk for a while now, remember?"

"Right. I'm still going to kick his ass, though. I thought you said he was working out?"

Jaeger shrugged. "That's what he told me. I didn't know about this either. I'm not going to distract him right now, though. That Torski looks..." His words trailed off as he took a better look at the fight unfolding. *"Fraxx.* Does he look high to you?"

Cynder narrowed her eyes and focused on the big alien. "He's...something. If I didn't know better, I'd say he was on red-rage levels of *crimson.* Does that stuff even work on Torskis?"

Toro connected with a punch that would have dropped a Nantari rhino, but his opponent shook it off and came back for more. For the first time in his life, Jaeger felt a pang of concern for his brother. This wasn't a fight Toro could win. Not on his own. "Based on what we're seeing, I'd say the answer is yes. I'm going in there. There's no way T is going to be able to subdue him without help."

"You're going to fight?" she asked, eyes wide with surprise.

"I have to. That's my brother in there."

"I'll come, too— son of a starbeast! What's *he* doing here?" Cyn's attention wasn't on the fight anymore. He couldn't tell who she was reacting to, but her anger was obvious. "I've got a hunch I know who the *crimson* dealer is."

"Go. I've got T. You call in security, and tell them we're going to need medical for the Torski, too."

She took off through the crowd, and both of them called out to the other at the same time, "Watch your ass!"

Jaeger didn't wait to see where Cyn was going. She could take care of herself. Toro was the one who needed his help.

He forced his way through the crowd, leaving bruised and disgruntled patrons in his wake. He made it to the edge of the pit and took a second to assess the action below. Toro's lip was split and bleeding, and he was limping slightly, but he was still on his feet.

"I'm coming in. On your six." He sent the brief message to Toro, then hopped the fence and

dropped into the fighting pit a few feet behind T. In the time it took him to make the leap, he shifted gears and became the one thing he swore he would never be again: a soldier. Instincts and abilities he had done his best to forget or deny surged to the forefront of his mind. It was terrifying how easily the change came over him, how fast the man faded into the background, leaving only the killer.

"Just like old times, huh?" Toro said aloud, circling left while Jaeger started moving to the right.

"Yeah. Only this time I'm the one saving your ass."

Toro scoffed. "You haven't saved anything, yet. Don't count your Torskis before they're out cold."

Jaeger snickered.

"Shut up, that sounded better in my head."

"Maybe it should have stayed there," he replied. It was part of their ritual. They never stopped talking when they were in a fight. The worse the odds, the more they bantered.

A glass of something blue and foamy crashed at his feet, sending shards of glass and liquid flying. "*Fraxxing* cyborgs are cheating!" Someone shouted.

The Torski bellowed and charged at Jaeger, who ducked an incoming haymaker and then sidestepped the stampeding alien.

"I don't think they're happy to see you in here with me, Jaeg." Toro closed in and slammed several rapid-fire punches to the back of the

Torski's head. If they could disorient it, they could subdue him before one of them got seriously hurt.

"Maybe we should send your big friend up there and see how they feel then?" Jaeger said before performing a leg sweep that almost took the big alien down. Enraged and off-balance, the Torski windmilled his arms in a desperate attempt to stay upright, but Toro landed a powerful kick to the center of his chest, sending the alien crashing to the floor.

They both pounced on him, working together to subdue the thrashing, enraged alien. By the time Toro managed to get him in a chokehold, both of them were battered, bruised, and under verbal attack from the angry onlookers above. Another glass was thrown, this one narrowly missing Toro's head before shattering against the wall of the pit.

"This is getting ugly. Where's Cyn?" Toro asked when the Torski finally stopped fighting them and lapsed into unconsciousness.

"Hopefully, she's calling Corp-Sec and a medical team."

"She's not one to miss out on a good fight; I figured she'd be joining us."

Jaeger shook his head. "If I know our girl, she's kicking someone else's ass right now. She went after someone she thought was a *crimson* dealer. At least, I think that's what she said. Things happened fast once we figured out you were in here with a whacked out opponent. Why the *fraxx* are you in here, anyway?"

Toro gave him a bloody grin that started his split lip bleeding again. "Draxx offered me a wad of scrip to fill in for one of his fighters. I bought Cyn a present. Something nice. You know, to celebrate."

"Be sure to give it to her fast. Maybe it will save you from her kicking your tail for fighting outside the Nova."

The doors to the pit opened, and several Corp-Sec officers came rushing in, followed by a medical team. More security appeared and surrounded the pit. They had things in hand quickly, dispersing the crowd with efficiency while the medical team started working on the three fighters.

He waved them off. "I'm a cyborg. I'll heal. Focus on the big guy, I don't know how much *crimson* is in his system, but it's a hell of a lot."

Toro got to his feet with a grunt then wandered over to help Jaeger up. "You okay?"

Jaeger knew he was asking about more than just his fresh collection of cuts and bruises. There had been a time he would have been angry at having to break his vow, but that was another life. One before Cynder. Before he had finally started to forgive himself for his past. Cyn was right. He couldn't pick and choose which of their actions to forgive. It was an all or nothing deal. "I'm good. You?"

Toro shrugged. "Nothing that won't heal in a few hours. I think that big bastard cracked a couple of ribs and tenderized my insides pretty good, but the medi-bots will handle it." He wrapped Jaeger into a one-armed hug that made both men wince. "I know what it meant for you to get into the pit with me today. Thank you. If you hadn't…"

"I will always have your back, T. Always. You and Cyn are all that matters. Besides, it was way past time I turned the tables and saved your ass."

"I'm glad both your sexy asses are still in one piece," Cyn commented from her vantage point above them. She was leaning on the railing, not a hair out of place and looking very pleased with herself.

"Hey, sugar."

She arched a brow at Toro. "Don't you 'hey, sugar,' me. You're late for our dinner date, and your choice of venues leaves a lot to be desired. Not to mention, you look like hell. You're not really going to take me to dinner looking like that, are you?"

Jaeger looked up at her and winked. "You got something else in mind, beautiful?"

"We give our statements, sign our names, and then find a hotel that offers room service. How's that sound?"

"It sounds like Toro's paying for an upgrade on our vacation."

T frowned, opened his mouth, then sighed. "Yeah, okay. That's fair."

"Come on up here. I've convinced Corp-Sec to let us have a drink while we give our statements." She blew them a kiss and vanished from the railing.

Damn, he loved that woman.

"She's something else, isn't she?" Toro asked.

"She really is. This present you got her. What is it?" he asked.

"Diamonds."

"Son of a bitch. So, it's going to be like that, is it?"

Toro chuckled and patted his pocket. "Next time, we'll buy her something together. Like, maybe…a ring?"

A ring. The ultimate claim a man could make on a woman. A promise of forever wrought in precious metals and gems. "It will have to be something special."

"We'll find something one of a kind. Just like her."

* * * *

Cynder was more than ready for their security interviews, with all their stupid, repetitive questions, to come to an end. Her drink was gone, and her attempt to order another one while still being questioned had raised the eyebrows of the two Corp-Sec officers speaking to her. They were young, and it was evident by their body language and questioning that they didn't have any love for cyborgs. It had been a long, frustrating hour for all of them. When she got back home, she was going to have a word with Mack and Dash about the way she had been treated. The dealer, Vesker, was a lowlife waste of good oxygen, but he was human, and apparently that made all the difference to these two.

"We're nearly done here, only one more thing I want to go over again. I need you to explain exactly why you believed Vesker Tarn was dealing unregistered pharma, specifically the pharmaceutical known as *crimson*."

This was the fifth time the rookie officer had asked her to justify why she'd gone after Vesker, and she was tired of explaining herself. She decided it was time to cut the bullshit. "Give me your data tablet." She held out her hand to the young man who gawked at her.

"What? No."

"I'm tired of answering the same questions over and over. You clearly don't know what cyborg recall is, so I've decided it's faster to show you than to sit here for another hour. Give me your tablet, please. Then we can all get the *fraxx* out of here."

"I'm trying to be thorough. You could be up on charges of assault, you know. The man you went after has a broken wrist and several bruised ribs from when you were trying to *subdue* him."

She snorted with disdain. "I told him if I ever saw him dealing unregistered pharma again, I'd toss him out the nearest airlock. All things considered, he's lucky all he has is a busted wrist. Give me the tablet, and I'll show you what I saw."

He handed her the data tablet. "How are you going to show me what you saw?"

"You have a lot to learn about cyborgs." She took the tablet and placed her hand over the input terminal. Data transfer wasn't something they liked doing. Connecting to a computer was not a comfortable sensation, and it gave the humans yet another reason to think of them as machines instead of living beings.

It took mere seconds to copy the pertinent data and move it onto the tablet. "There you go, a visual record of everything I saw Vesker doing tonight, including the part where he tried to knock me unconscious with a baton. I bet he didn't mention that while he was screaming that I attacked him for no reason."

The officer took the tablet back, his brow furrowed and his lips pressed into a thin line as he activated the file she had loaded onto the tablet. "You can do that? Just, give me your memories?"

"Yeah, we can all do that. Don't they teach you anything before they issue you the uniform? If you're done here, do you think you could let our girlfriend go? She's given you everything you need," Toro said from somewhere behind her. His voice, while pleasant, had a cool undertone that made it clear he wasn't really asking their permission.

"Why didn't you tell me you could do that? Did you know they could do that?" the officer asked his partner, who shook his head.

"Like I said, you have a lot to learn about cyborgs. Lesson number one, if you treat us like human beings and not freaks, we're much more cooperative." She tapped her ear. "We have excellent hearing, too. I heard what you said when you got sent over here to interview me."

The officer had the decency to look chagrined. "I'll remember that in future. All of it." He watched the images play for a few more seconds, freezing it when he spotted Vesker holding a handful of distinctive red ampules he was handing off to customers. "You're free to go. If we have any further questions—"

Jaeger cut him off. "If you have more questions, you can ask them tomorrow. Better yet, send them to the head of the *crimson* Task Force on Astek station. We'll give our answers to them."

They were out of the bar two minutes later. They swung by the hotel, packed their things, and checked out. She had been stuck in her interview long enough for Jaeg and T to arrange for new accommodations.

The three of them made quite a sight as they wandered into the lobby of the five-star establishment. Both men were healing quickly, but their clothes were still disheveled and bloody. The desk clerk rushed through their check-in, no doubt hoping to get them to their room and out of sight before they unsettled the delicate sensibilities of the other guests.

Their room was a thing of beauty. Plush cream carpets were deep enough they left footprints behind when they walked. The furniture was all curlicues and polished wood, and even the air was sweet and pure. They must have a powerful, in-house air purifying system in place, scrubbing away all trace of the world beyond the doors of the hotel.

"Holy *fraxx*. If you can afford this, I'm paying you too much," she exclaimed as she prowled around the suite, checking out everything.

"You're worth it," Toro replied.

"How about we take turns cleaning up while I order up room service?" Jaeger suggested.

"Sounds perfect. I'm volunteering as shower assistant for you both." She was already shedding her clothes as she made her way to the breathtaking expanse of marble and tile that was their bathroom. It was a hell of an upgrade. Then again, her whole day had been like that. Her day had started in a place of loneliness, anger, and pain, and it was ending with joy, love, and laughter…and a dash of brawling and bruises. In her world, that was pretty much a fairytale ending.

Toro finished the last of his meal and leaned back against the polished wooden headboard of their massive bed. The satin finish of the wood felt good against his bare back, and he idly wondered what it would cost to buy something like it for himself. It was decadence, sure, but he was starting to develop an appreciation for the finer things in life. Especially if he could buy them for Cynder.

None of them had bothered getting fully dressed after their showers. He and Jaeger had tossed on loose, drawstring pants they usually reserved for working out, while Cyn was only wearing an oversized t-shirt that hung almost to her knees. They were all sprawled on the bed amid the remnants of their meal, which had turned into a makeshift picnic that reminded him of their first date. "That was incredible. I'm not even sure it's legal to serve food that good."

"Do you think they'd notice if I kidnapped their entire kitchen staff and took them back to the Nova with us? If we had that kind of talent in the kitchen, we'd have a full house every night," Cyn said.

"Kidnapping is on Corp-Sec's no-no list. I don't advise it." Jaeger started clearing away the dishes, stacking them on the cart room service had left.

Cynder sighed. "Yeah, I should probably avoid annoying them for a while after today. Who knew they'd get so cranky over a broken wrist? The asshole tried to club me, I was defending myself."

"How'd that happen, anyway? I thought the plan was for you to call in Corp-Sec and watch the little weasel, not take him down yourself." Jaeger said.

"He spotted me and bolted. Guilty men don't run, and by that point, I'd already seen him dealing *crimson*, anyway. I know Mack and Dash haven't made any progress figuring out how the pharma is coming into the Drift. That dealer you tipped them off about wasn't high enough level to be of any use, and I was hoping Vesker could have answers the taskforce needs. I want that shit out of my club and off the Drift. It's already put two people I care about in danger."

She turned toward him and glowered. "Speaking of which, what were you doing at the Pit today? Why did you leave our room, T? I woke up, and you were gone."

Guilt danced across Toro's heart wearing stiletto heels. "I'm sorry about that. I shouldn't have left. I was still on edge after everything, and I figured I'd go burn off some energy and be back before you woke up."

"I think we've done enough leaving each other for a while, don't you?" she asked, her voice softer now.

"It won't happen again." He rose from the bed and jammed a hand into his pocket, looking for the gift he bought. He had been waiting for the right time to give it to her and now seemed the perfect moment. Nothing said, "I'm sorry I screwed up," quite like jewelry. At least, that's what he had always heard.

"Going somewhere?" she asked.

"Not without you." He pulled out the box, gripping it tightly as he struggled to find the right words. "I fought today because Draxx offered me a lot of scrip to fill a hole in the roster. I said yes because I wanted to buy you something special. Something to mark this day. I know it started out lousy, but it ended pretty well. Us together. Loving each other. And well, here." He offered the box to her on his upturned palm.

"You bought me a present?"

She sat up, a move that made the t-shirt she had stolen from his bag ride up her thighs. He forced himself to tear his eyes away from the tempting sight of all that bare skin to watch her reaction to his gift. She took the box slowly, letting her fingers caress his hand as she pulled away, her eyes never leaving the small package in her hands.

"That's okay, isn't it? I mean, that I bought you something?" he asked. She was acting funny. Like she wasn't sure what to make of things.

She lifted her gaze to his, revealing the tears glittering on her lashes. "It's so much more than okay. No one's ever done this for me. I mean, we exchange presents on major holidays and stuff, but nobody has ever bought me a gift just because they wanted to."

Jaeger sat down on the bed beside her, his hand settling on her hip. "That's going to change, now, beautiful."

"Everything is changing," she said and opened the lid of her gift.

A soft gasp fell from her lips as she stared at the pair of earrings nestled inside. They were black diamond studs set with emerald chips that had reminded him of Cynder's green eyes.

"They're beautiful!" she launched herself at him, beaming.

Her response was everything he hoped for. He caught her in his arms and crushed her to him, his mouth slanting over hers. He didn't kiss so much as devour her, the cinnamon and sugar taste of her lips and the heat of her mouth carving themselves into his memory forever. She coiled herself around him, her arms around his neck, her long legs wrapping around his waist as he fell back on the mattress, taking her with him.

His lower lip was still healing after the fight, but the small twinges of pain were nothing compared to the pleasure of having her in his arms. He would have to be dead not to want her, and even then, he would probably be haunting her, hoping for one last kiss.

He flipped them over, pinning her beneath him. Her legs were still twined around his waist, pulling him snug against her exposed pussy. Heat seared the length of his already hard cock, and his control threatened to snap when she arched her hips and ground their bodies together.

"Something you want, sugar?" he asked.

"You," she murmured. She turned her head to look at Jaeger, her eyes glowing with desire and joy. "Both of you."

"I think that can be arranged," he said, aware that Jaeger was already stripping off his pants, eager to join in.

"Like you could keep me away," Jaeger retorted.

Cyn wriggled beneath him, fighting to get her shirt over her head while still pinned to the mattress. Every wiggle and twist made his cock throb, and by the time she was done, he was ready to combust with need. She knew it, too; he could tell by the wicked gleam in her eyes as she stared up at him.

Jaeger took the box from her hand and set the earrings on the side table, though he uttered a low whistle of admiration first. "Nice choice, T. Classy and a little dark, just like our woman."

"Dark. Really?" she asked, her green eyes flashing.

"Mhmm. Mysterious, dangerous, and dark."

"And maybe a little bit violent," Toro added.

"I don't know whether to be flattered or insulted." She flexed her fingers, scratching her nails down the back of his neck.

"I love that you're dangerous. It's sexy. We've all been through hell. If you didn't have a little darkness in you, how could you ever understand the darkness in us?" Jaeger asked as he leaned in to steal a kiss from Cynder.

She moaned and moved a hand from Toro's shoulder to Jaeger's, drawing him in for a deeper kiss. Toro took advantage of her distraction to pull free of her legs. Not that he wanted to move, but he needed to ditch his pants. There would be no need for any of them to be dressed for the rest of the night.

Cynder couldn't keep track of all the emotions bubbling up inside her: Joy, love, happiness, desire, and so many more. The grief, confusion, and doubt were gone. All of it wiped away because of the two men who had found a way past her defenses and into her heart. She uttered a sigh of complete contentment and let herself be wrapped up in the arms of her men. Their warmth surrounded her, their solid strength a comfort she had missed in the short time they had been apart.

They were stretched out on either side of her, bracketing her between their hard bodies as they stroked and kissed every inch of her. It was intoxicating to be the center of their attention.

"Not the center of our attention, beautiful. You're the center of our world, now," Jaeger said.

She hadn't realized she had spoken her last thought aloud. Intoxicating was the right word for what they were doing to her if she was screwing up her inside and outside voices without even realizing it.

"I like it. Being the center of your world. I've never felt like this before." She reached out to lay a possessive hand on each of them.

"How do you feel, Cyn?" Toro asked, settling his big hand over hers.

"Happy. Only it's more than that. I know you said that you liked my dark side, but right now, I don't have one. You took all my darkness away."

Both men looked at her with adoration.

"Yeah?" Toro asked, as proud as if he had single-handedly slain a star dragon for her.

"Yeah." She slid her hands lower, stroking her way down to their cocks with obvious intent. "I think we should celebrate today. All of it."

They were hard as hull plating beneath her fingers, and both of them groaned in agreement.

"Whatever you want, beautiful."

"However you want it," Toro added.

Her heart sped up to light speed as she whispered her next words. "Together. I want the two of you to take me, together."

They both spoke at once.

"*Fraxx*. You mean—" Toro blurted out.

"Are you sure?" Jaeger asked.

"I'm sure. I've never done it. I want to try, though." She blushed. "Zura might have mentioned it. She said it was incredible."

Both men were silent for a short span, and then Jaeger cleared his throat. "We've never done that, either."

The answer surprised her. She assumed there wasn't much the two of them hadn't tried. After all, they'd been on their own for years. Most cyborgs she knew had jumped into the deep end of the sex and playtime pool the moment they had been freed.

"Then let's do this together. Something special between the three of us."

"Everything with you is special," Toro said before leaning in to kiss her. He ran his tongue over the seam of her lips, and she parted them, letting him inside. His kiss was heat, and strength, and breathless intensity all blended together into one intense package.

While her focus was on Toro, Jaeger moved out of her sight, and the next thing she knew he was at her feet, pressing a string of soft kisses along her instep up to her ankle. He cradled her heel in one hand as he kissed his way higher, the feather-light touch of his mouth and the light scratch of his beard a shocking contrast to Toro's hard, demanding kisses.

Sensing her distraction, Toro nipped her lower lip and then ended their kiss. "Meet you in the middle?" he asked Jaeger before lowering his head to her throat.

"Brilliant plan," Jaeger replied.

Toro worked down her body an inch at a time, leaving no part of her untouched or untasted. When he reached her breasts, he uttered a groan before drawing one hard nipple into his mouth. When his teeth closed around the tender nub, pleasure tore through her; sparks of need ignited her blood, making her clit throb and swell.

Jaeger's laughter buzzed against her calf as he laid a trail of kisses up her leg, heading for her knee. When he got there, he turned his head and swiped his tongue over the tender flesh there. She opened her legs wider, giving him room to settle his broad shoulders between her thighs. Warm silk sheets beneath her, the heated touch of two mouths and two pairs of hands on her body, the scent of sex perfuming the air. This was heaven, or as close to it as she could imagine. This was where she was supposed to be, and she would never turn away from them again.

Jaeger was only a few inches from her pussy when he raised his head, depriving her of his touch. Toro stopped at almost the same time. Jaeger rose to his knees, while Toro seated himself by her hip before stroking his hand down her stomach with one calloused hand. He delved into her slick folds, going straight for the swollen bundle of nerves tucked away beneath its delicate hood. She arched her hips, pressing herself against his fingers, then gasped as Jaeger joined in, sliding a digit deep into her channel.

They worked her in concert, driving her to the heights of pleasure. Jaeger added a second finger, curving them to stroke over her sweet spot with every thrust. Soon she was lost in a maelstrom of sensation, every touch sending her closer to the brink.

"Come for us, Cyn. I want to see you come apart, and then we're going to take you somewhere you've never been before. All of us, together, just like you asked. Me in your sweet pussy while T takes you from behind," Jaeger whispered.

His sexually charged words flowed over her like an invisible caress. The image of the three of them together sent her hurtling into an orgasm so strong that her next breath caught in her lungs as she arched off the bed.

They continued their sensual onslaught, stretching out her release until she was panting and trembling between them. She was overloaded on bliss, her limbs heavy, and her heart pounding as they took her to her limits and then pushed past them.

They gave her a brief moment to recover while both of them moved around the bed. By the time her senses were unscrambled, and she was back in control of her limbs, Toro was stretched out on his side, facing her.

"Will you wear these for me?" he asked, holding out the diamonds.

"Happily." She held out her hand, and he gave them to her, watching with rapt attention as she put them on.

"You naked is amazing. You naked and wearing diamonds is *fraxxing* incredible," he said, his gaze hot enough to rival the heart of a star.

"I've never been much for jewelry, but if you're going to look at me that way every time I wear some, I'm going to start wearing it more often."

Toro nodded. "I like that plan. I'm going to need to start fighting more often, maybe work more security shifts, too."

"Why?" She asked, not following his logic.

Jaeger chuckled. "I think T's got a new hobby. Buying you shiny things for you to wear while naked. I know that look, Cyn. You're going to wind up draped in jewels from the top of your head to your cute little toes."

"Hell yes. That's my new goal in life." Toro looked over at Jaeger. "And don't pretend I'm the only one who thinks she looks like a goddess right now. You know you're going to be shopping, too."

"You don't need to buy me things, guys."

"Need? No. Want to? Yes. We've got minimal expenses and nothing else to spend it on. Why shouldn't we buy you things to make all of us happy?" Toro asked. His brows were knitted, and his jaw was tense, two clear signs he wasn't happy with her response.

"You have a future to save up for. Plans...." She waved her hand in a vague motion above her. "Don't you?"

"The only future we're planning for is you, beautiful," Jaeger said, taking her hand in his and squeezing it.

"Only you," Toro added.

Her heart stuttered, and when it resumed its normal beat, the world had shifted around her. "I love you two so much."

Jaeger drank in the sight of the woman he loved as she lay between them wearing nothing but diamonds and a smile. Toro was a genius. She did look like a goddess. Their goddess. He leaned in for a quick kiss, savoring the taste of her lips before lying down on his back beside her.

All he had to do was crook a finger, and she came to him, straddling his waist with her long legs. Her hands came down on either side of his face, and she lowered herself until her breasts brushed his chest. He speared a hand into her hair, tugging her down until she was close enough to kiss. She moaned against his lips as a shiver passed through her, and a fresh flood of cream soaked his cock where it lay pressed to her pussy. He loved how responsive she was. Every touch of their hands or mouths drew a reaction that threw rocket fuel on the flames already burning inside him.

"Hi," she murmured, staring into his eyes as she rocked her body over his.

"Hey, beautiful. You ready for this?" he asked.

She nodded, and there was nothing but trust and love in her eyes. "Love me."

Mouths mated first, locked together in a kiss that sizzled across his soul. She took him into her body in one eager arch of her hips. He gripped her hips and drove himself deep, lifting them both off the bed.

Toro moved into place behind her, kneeling between Jaeger's legs. Neither of them had done this before, but that didn't mean they hadn't talked about it. It was a fantasy come to life, sharing a woman's body so intimately.

He did all he could to keep Cynder's focus on him, fucking her with slow, steady thrusts while his tongue danced with hers. Her breath was in his lungs, the delicate musk of her scent hung in the air between them, her soft skin rubbing against his.

Toro sent him a single word via their internal comms, letting him know he was ready. A second later, Cyn moaned and stiffened, then relaxed again.

"That's right," Toro said, his tone as soft as Jaeger had ever heard it. "This is going to be good, Cyn. So long as we take it slow."

"Slow might kill me, but he's right." Jaeger took hold of her hips, coaxing her back into a slow, rocking rhythm he knew she liked. Her moans grew louder, and soon she was moving between them in mindless pleasure.

"Oil is going to feel a little cool," Toro said.

That got her attention. Cyn's head snapped up, and she turned to look back at T. "You brought lube with you?"

Jaeger chuckled. "No. They stocked some massage oil in the bathroom samples along with the shampoos and soaps."

"Oh. I missed that."

"You were admiring the marble shower at the time," Toro said.

"I was. I think I want one back home," she said.

"We'll make that happen. What our lady wants, she gets. Right, Jaeg?"

"Damn right."

She laughed. It was a deep–throated chuckle that was as sensuous as it was joyful. The laugh morphed into a moan as Toro worked his fingers deeper, the pressure of his touch strong enough for Jaeger to feel against his cock. It was an unexpected but seductive sensation that made his balls tighten as ribbons of desire coiled deep in his gut.

The three of them continued their dance, learning the steps as they went until Toro paused and lifted his gaze to meet Jaeger's. It was time.

Jaeger slipped his hand between them, pushing along sweat-slickened skin until he found her clit. Her hips bucked against his fingers then stilled as Toro pressed himself inside. Jaeger felt the invasion, the breathtaking tightness that overtook him as they both claimed her for their own.

Time stopped as the three of them adjusted, but then Cynder wriggled her hips experimentally, and both he and Toro groaned.

"If you do that again, I'm not going to be able to go slow," Toro warned.

"I don't want slow. I want this. Please."

"As we've already discussed, what milady wants, she gets," Jaeger said, and Toro grunted in agreement.

Cynder rocked her hips forward, taking Jaeger deeper and setting the pace for a new dance.

"You're so tight right now," T groaned, then rolled his hips, burying himself inside her.

They began to move together, finding their way into a give and take that felt like it could go on forever. Pleasure built upon pleasure until he lost himself in a sea of sensations. The sound of their breathing, the slick slap of skin on skin, the smell of sex, and the murmured whispers of passion all blended together into one perfect moment. The pace accelerated, her pussy clenching tight around his cock until he could barely breathe.

When she came, it was with their names on her lips. Every shudder and flex of her body milked their cocks, and within seconds, he joined her in orgasm. He was still in the throes of ecstasy when Toro threw back his head and roared.

Cynder dropped onto his chest with a satisfied moan, and Toro collapsed on top of her, pressing them both down into the mattress. It was a closeness he had never experienced before, all of them tangled together.

"*Fraxx*, that was amazing," Toro muttered. "You still with us, Cyn?"

"Slightly shattered and a little squished, but I'm still here."

"Sorry." Toro moved, easing himself away from them both.

"Never be sorry for that. I'd rather be caught between the two of you than anywhere else in all the worlds."

"That's where we want you to be. Always." Jaeger brushed a hand over her cheek, and she nuzzled into his chest. Somewhere in the background he heard the sound of running water and knew that Toro was cleaning up. They'd take care of Cynder, and then the three of them were going to rest before doing it all again. Tonight, and for the rest of their lives.

EPILOGUE

Last call was done, and the final few patrons were meandering their way to the door when Cynder finally called her night done. She claimed a chair at an empty table near the main bar with a tired groan and grabbed a handful of popcorn from the bag she'd filled on her last patrol of the club. It had been a busy night. In the days since returning from her impromptu vacation, there had been a lot of busy nights.

The Pit had never re-opened after the night of Toro's fight with the Torski. It turned out that the owner, Draxx, was working with the Drojo Cartel. He was letting them use his bar as a funnel for *crimson*, bringing it in disguised as inventory. Corp-Sec shut him down, and before she left Torex platform, she had successfully negotiated contracts with the best of his fighters, adding them to the Nova's stable. The extra fighters meant more fights, more customers, and more income for the club.

"Luke. Hit me. I don't care what it is as long as it's cold and wet," she called over to her brother. He was still behind the bar, helping the bartenders clean up.

"You got it."

"Make that two, please." Zura joined Cyn at the table, dropping into a chair with her usual grace. Her sister-in-law might only be half Pheran, but she had inherited the species' cat-like grace along with their stunning blue coloring.

"Two Sun Sprite's Delights, coming up."

Zura's silver eyes gleamed with pleasure as she blew a kiss to her husband. "Thank you."

"I still can't believe he named a cocktail after your ship instead of you," Cyn muttered in mocking tones.

"He's promised the next one will be named for me." Zura leaned back in her chair and grinned at her. "My guys aren't as naturally romantic as yours."

Cyn reached up to touch her diamond earrings, then let her hand fall to the black gold choker chain that encircled her throat. "They're spoiling me." Her voice dropped to a confessional whisper. "I love it."

"You deserve to be spoiled. I'm glad you gave yourself a chance to be happy." She leaned in. "Have you heard anything more from Dr. Jefferies? She said she had something to tell you, but she wouldn't tell me what it was. Was it good news?"

Cyn shrugged and set the popcorn down on the table. "It was more of an update. She's still working on a way to undo what was done, but she is certain it's reversible. She's got a theory on why it was done, too."

Zura's nodded. "She mentioned that to me. She believes the corporations are worried about you and the other cyborg women passing your medi-bots on to your offspring."

Of course, the doctor would have spoken to Zura about it. She carried medi-bots in her bloodstream, too. The only non-cyborg any of them knew about who did. It was another medical mystery Dr. Jefferies was working to solve.

"It never occurred to me, but it does make sense. It's only a theory for now, though."

"If she's right, the corporations aren't going to like it if I get pregnant. They can't do to me what they did to you and the others." Zura's fingers drummed the tabletop, the sound loud enough to carry in the near silence of the club.

"You're fretting again. I told you not to. We're not going to let anything happen to you." Luke arrived, set down their drinks, and then bent down to kiss the top of his wife's head.

"They wouldn't stand a snowball's chance in a supernova of getting close to you. You've got three big, bad, cyborgs watching over you, little blue. If you ever make me an aunt, you know I wouldn't let anyone or anything threaten my family."

"Club's empty, and the doors are locked. Where are you right now?" Toro asked.

She was still getting used to being connected to both Toro and Jaeger via internal channels. Jaeger and the doctor had figured it out without too much trouble, and they'd made the link only a few days ago. Being connected to her lovers had made her reconsider other choices, and as a result, she had activated the channel between her and her brothers. The time for standing alone was over.

"We're by the bar. Want a drink?"

"Of course, he wants a drink. It's like you don't know us at all, beautiful." Jaeger wandered over from the direction of the gaming tables, wearing one of the new uniforms he had helped to develop. Things had changed for all of them in the last few weeks. Jaeger worked for the club now, overseeing the gaming tables and putting his gambling experience to work for them.

The first thing he had changed was the dress code. The dealers all wore tailored blue shirts with black vests, now. It made them stand out, and the more professional attire had set a new tone. Since the staff had started wearing them, there were fewer fights and disruptions in the gaming area. Profits were up, too. Jaeger's experience, combined with his enhanced senses, were a match for even the most talented cheats.

"I got you covered, Jaeg." Luke joined them, carrying a tray of drinks.

"Am I the only one still working?" Kit arrived next, looking around at all of them with amusement.

"You haven't been working for the last ten minutes. You've been doing what you always do, oh fearless leader, you were standing off to the side, supervising everyone else." She snapped off a sharp salute that ended with a decidedly unmilitary flourish and then turned to Jaeger. "Hey there, handsome. Care to be sexually harassed by your boss?"

"Always," he leaned in and kissed her until her brothers groaned in protest.

"Must you do that in front of us?" Luke grumbled.

"Yes, he must. I even put it in his contract."

"Tell me you didn't really do that," Kit said, frowning at the idea of his employees signing something like that.

"Oh yeah, she did. It's in the fine print, but it's there." Jaeger winked and kissed her again before snagging a beer off the table.

"The fine print? You talking about our contracts?" Toro asked as he arrived. He was a full-time security officer now, though he still fought from time to time. So did she, but now they were both doing it for fun, not income.

"She put something in your contract, too?" Luke asked, but unlike Kit, he was smirking with obvious amusement.

"Yep." Toro speared a hand into her hair, tugging her head. His kiss was hot enough to make her toes curl inside her combat boots.

"Do I want to know what it says?" Kit muttered.

"Probably not. They're very special contracts for my guys and no one else."

"Good. If you want to build a harem, do it on your own time." Kit arched a brow at Jaeger and Toro. "You really let her lock you two into long-term contracts?"

"Yeah. It comes with a hell of a benefits package. Fancy new rooms, better pay, and the hottest boss on the Drift." Jaeger took another pull on his beer then glanced over at Toro.

T nodded, and before she knew what was happening, they were both kneeling at her feet. The bar went completely silent as her employees, friends, and family materialized around them, all of them smiling. She caught sight of Royan, Zura's brother, along with Dash, Mack, and even Alyson. Everyone she knew was gathered around, waiting.

"You know we've signed on with the Nova Club as employees. Now, we want to make you an offer of our own. We're looking to lock you in forever, Cyn. With the most binding contract of all. Will you marry us?" Jaeger asked, looking up at her with love and a yearning that took her breath away.

"We want forever with you. Say yes," Toro added. He handed Jaeger a box, who opened it before offering it to her.

The tears in her eyes made it hard to see, and she had to blink a couple of times before she could focus on what was inside the red velvet box. It was a square-cut black diamond, flanked by a pair of smaller, square-cut sapphires and set in a ring of white gold. It was the most beautiful thing she had ever seen. She reached for it, only to have Jaeger move the box back away from her.

"You're supposed to say yes, first, then take the ring," Jaeger prompted her in a dramatic whisper.

"Uh…oh!" She tore her eyes from the ring to find both men staring at her with love and anticipation. "Of course, the answer is yes! Yes, I'll marry you. Yes, I want forever with you, too."

The bar erupted into cheers and catcalls. Toro grasped her hands and tugged her off the chair into his lap, kissing her happily.

"You had me worried for a second, sugar."

She threw her arms around him and held on tight. Toro was her rock. His love was a constant thing, guiding her through the dark moments and helping her stay on course. "I love you," she whispered against his lips, ignoring the taste of her tears as they spilled down her cheeks to wet flavor their kiss.

"You were the only woman to ever see who I was and accept it. I'm glad we found you."

Jaeger took the box from her hand and plucked the ring from it. He set it on her left hand and held tight until she was ready to let go of Toro. When she turned to him, he kissed her too, his mouth tender against hers, his thumb sweeping away the tracks of her tears from her face. Jaeg, the smooth talker who hid his darkness under a glossy veneer. He was the one who could always make her smile, even when he was weary from fighting his own battles.

"You are a miracle. Our miracle. The one woman in the galaxy who could make us both whole again and then encourage us to become so much more. I don't know what the future will bring, but I will promise you this: whatever the corporations have done, no matter what happens or what we find out, we'll face it together, like a family should. I love you, Cyn."

More tears fell, but she didn't care who saw them. Not this time. "I love you, too, Diceman. I always will."

They were surrounded then, caught up in a flurry of hugs and back slaps and congratulations that continued until her head spun, and her heart was nearly overflowing with love and laughter.

She joined her men, wrapping an arm around them both. "So, when are we getting married?"

"How about right now?" Phyl asked, her voice carrying over the din.

"You can do that?" Toro asked, bemused.

"Sweetie, I can do a lot of things, and some of them are even legal. Yes, I can marry the three of you. You'll have to be on my ship to do it, but I *am* a captain, and that's one of the best perks of the job."

Cynder released her men to hug Phyl, lifting her off her feet. "Yes please."

Phyl grunted. "If you break my ribs, girl, you're not getting married tonight. Put me down without snapping me in two then get your asses over to the *Beacon*. We'll have you married in no time."

Cynder grabbed Toro and Jaeger by the hands and made for the door of the bar. "Come on, guys. The last time I was on the *Beacon*, I was running away from you. This time, I'm going to vow never to go anywhere without you, ever again."

The gathered in the cargo hold of Phyl's ship a few minutes later. Everyone she knew was there. Even the ones not working that night. That was all she needed for her wedding day. She didn't need a fancy dress or flowers or a party. Everything she needed was right here.

She looked around and saw her brothers hugging Zura and watching with smiles on their faces. Everything she ever wanted had finally come to her: friends, family, love, and a chance to live a full life. She was going to take what she had been given and run with it. She would enjoy every second, not just for herself, but for Dana, too, and all the others they'd lost in their dark journey to freedom.

As she spoke the words that would tie her to Toro and Jaeger for the rest of her life, she couldn't stop smiling. She may not have believed in happily ever after, but it looked like she was getting one, anyway. In her heart, she knew her sister had some part in making all this happen. Dana had always been the one who believed in fairy tale endings.

Thanks, sis. Wherever you are, I hope you're happy, too. With that thought, she finally found the strength to let go of the past. It was time to look ahead to the future, the one she would share with the men standing at her side.

The End

ABOUT THE AUTHOR

Susan lives out on the Canadian west coast surrounded by open water, dear family, and good friends. She's jumped out of perfectly good airplanes on purpose and accidently swum with sharks on the Great Barrier Reef.

If the world ends, she plans to survive as the spunky, comedic sidekick to the heroes of the new world, because she's too damned short and out of shape to make it on her own for long.

To contact her about her books or to arrange end of the world team-ups, you can email her at *susan@susanhayes.ca*.

For all titles by Susan Hayes, please visit her website: **susanhayes.ca**

To keep up with her latest news, releases, and appearances you can join her Newsletter: http://eepurl.com/bd_GoH

THE DRIFT SERIES

Double Down

All in